Ramblin

with

JOHN ROBINS

A Dartmoor Miscellany of
Explorations, Reminiscences
and a Fantasy Tale of
a Vanishing Valley

For my Dartmoor friends
DAVID & JOHN, KATHY & DAVE,
TOM, COLIN, PETER.
Old Uncle Tom Cobley and all.

Best wishes
John Robins

Acknowledgements

Text

Some of the material in this book has appeared either in the Dartmoor Magazine or Tamar Journal. It is reproduced here with the kind permission and courtesy of their Editors.

Plates

All photographs by the author unless otherwise stated.

Maps

All maps specially drawn by the author. Map 4 is adapted from an aerial photograph by kind permission of West Air Photography CA of Weston-Super-Mare.

First published in 1988 by
JOHN PEGG PUBLISHING
47 High Street,
Pembury,
Kent TN2 4PH.

ISBN 0 9508598 9 3

John Pegg Publishing

Printed in Great Britain by The Signal Press Ltd.,
137 Great Suffolk Street, London SE1 1PP.

Contents

List of Photographs

List of Photographs

List of Maps

Preface

In the conclusion of my book "Follow the Leat" I wrote "I am quite sure that by the time this book gets into print I shall wish that I had incorporated this fact or that finding." That has proved even more prophetic than I had supposed. With further reading, discussions amongst friends, and a lot more walking and investigating, I have collected so much of interest it seems a pity not to make it available to all those fellow lovers of Dartmoor who value its history. This is now made possible by the encouragement and cooperation of my dear friends David Edgley and John Pegg, who have undertaken the onerous task of publication.

However, in these walks of exploration, the purpose has been to find plausible explanations from the available evidence and what remains to be seen on the ground. In my interpretations I am offering opinions, not stating facts. Further evidence may come to light which may modify these opinions. The reader must go out and look for himself and form his own conclusions. It would not surprise me to find that they differ from mine, just as I find I differ from what other authors have written.

Looking back over the years of discovering Dartmoor there are certain walks which have a special significance for me and stand out in my memory more clearly than others. I include some of these because I think they help to explain how the Moor grows on one, until it eventually becomes an all-absorbing passion, a love never to be denied or forsaken, in spite of the harsh tricks and treatment it can play on one.

Finally I offer a little fantasy story, based on the history of a Dartmoor valley, which I had been contemplating for some years. It gave me so much pleasure in the writing of it, at a time when circumstances ordained that I could do nothing else worth while, that it is my hope that the reader will also get some enjoyment from it.

John Robins
Tavistock

PART ONE

A Nostalgic Account of some Memorable Walks

A Nostalgic Account of some Memorable Walks

I chose Tavistock as a place of retirement because of its proximity to Dartmoor, a decision that I have never regretted.

At that time, 1962, I only had a superficial knowledge of Dartmoor. As children we had spent many a holiday on or near the Moor, at Horrabridge, Clearbrook, and South Brent, and I remember them as very happy occasions, carefree and healthy. Tavistock I only knew as a place one passed through, but even those fleeting glimpses held attractive memories.

So, when the time came to retire from my work in Cable and Wireless, everything seemed to fall into place. Tavistock, little changed from the days of the 7th Duke of Bedford, who in the middle years of the nineteenth century was instrumental in the rebuilding of its centre, was just beginning to expand, with new estates being carved out of the property which subsequent dukes were forced to sell to meet crippling death duties. Deer Park Crescent was one of them, ideally suited to my needs and wishes and within my means. On 15th May 1962 we moved into our new home. Dartmoor was just next door.

My early walks were mostly exploratory, and of course thrilling when they led into unknown places, giving one a sense of adventure. Very often they were made early in the morning, sometimes before dawn, taking my breakfast with me. And this I can whole-heartedly recommend, for then one can really savour Dartmoor's unique atmosphere, the sense of freedom, wildness, peace, mystery, the dew beneath one's feet, a gentle cool breeze, the light gradually increasing from the east, and eventually the sun breaking clear of the early morning clouds to bring a little warmth and comfort. Animals peacefully grazing, the cheerful twittering of the lark, the call of the cuckoo. At such a time you have Dartmoor to yourself and you thank God for it.

It is not always like that of course, but that is how I like to remember it. So often the weather looks promising in Tavistock but by the time the top of Pork Hill is reached you are enveloped in fog. On one occasion I planned a walk from Lower Godsworthy, Peter Tavy, to Sandy Ford on the River Walkham. A broad stony path leads all the way to it, so I was not too worried by the early morning fog, which I felt sure would lift before long. But it still persisted as I passed Cocks Hill and approached the valley, and there an astonishing sight opened out before me. The sun had just risen and was shining through the mist giving an overall fiery red glow. I got the impression that I was descending into the jaws of Hades. It was a relief to reach the river and find it peacefully flowing and visibility somewhat improved, which encouraged me to continue along its banks down stream. At Shallow Ford I left it and took to the track which the map showed me should lead me back to the previous track I had been following, at a point near to the Longstone. After some time, the fog now just as thick as ever, I became aware of some ghostly shapes on my left. Humans? Sheep? or what? They materialised as a group of upright stones: I was beside the Langstone Stone Circle, and thus some way off my intended direction. My next hazard was a mire, the source of the Wedlake Brook, which I attempted to cross but soon thought better of it and made a long detour round its head, eventually regaining the track I had been aiming for. By which time, and perversely of course, the fog lifted and Dartmoor returned to normal.

Apart from this adventure, not too strong a word I feel for this period of my explorations, I can think of no other of my early walks that warrant any comment. From the very first I studied the maps of the Moor and learnt more about it by borrowing books from the Library, amongst them Crossing's Guide (original copies in more than one part) and various articles in the early editions of the Transactions of the Devonshire Association. In 1965 David and Charles brought out a reprint of Crossing's Guide, and soon afterwards Worth's "Dartmoor", two books which provided me with the knowledge and incentive to explore deeper into the lesser known areas of the Moor.

Around this time commenced the annual visits, in late June or early July, of Nancy Carver and Bernard Miller. Nancy, a cousin by marriage, had been a second mother to me when in 1922/23 I was a student at the Eastern Telegraph Company's Training School at Hampstead, London. I had spent many a happy weekend with her family at their home at East Sheen, within a few minutes walk of Richmond Park through which we had many a walk on a Sunday morning. I was more than glad now to repay some of that hospitality. Bernard was her nephew, and being orphaned early in his life, Nancy had mothered him also. We were both very fond of her. On Bernard's retirement from the Navy, and with Nancy now a widow, they had made a practice of spending their holidays together. And so it came about that the two of them came to us each year until Nancy's death in 1973, and then Bernard alone.

I always used to say that Bernard brought fine weather with him on these visits. Indeed I can think of very few days when we were not able to have a daily walk during their week-long stay. Bernard readily fell in with my practice of early morning walks. I would rouse him with a cup of tea and then make our breakfast sandwiches, one of bacon one of marmalade, and a flask of coffee each, and then we would set off as dawn was breaking. Our walks usually lasted for about four hours, so we were usually home in time to take the ladies out somewhere for a picnic lunch.

The Plym Valley

Some of my early walks were in search of prehistoric monuments. Drizzlecombe is famous for its tall menhirs and stone rows; I had visited them more than once. Beyond the plain the Plym valley narrows and disappears into the distance, but I had never ventured into it. So this became the purpose of one of our long walks together. I would not consider it long now, but then it was all new to us and appeared longer than it actually was. We could not have chosen a better day and I think this more than anything else made it memorable. To appreciate Dartmoor fully one should know it in all its temperamental moods, but there is little doubt that it looks its best on a fine sunny day, when cirrus and cumulus clouds break up the sky to give occasional respite from the heat of the sun and dapple the landscape with their shadows. This was such a day, when light clothing was all that was necessary, a gentle mellow breeze gave comfort and not a fly of any sort to torment us. Neither did we meet another human being throughout the walk to detract from its mystery and remoteness.

The walk commenced at Burracombe Gate, though the name was unknown to me then, not being marked on the map. A stony track led eastwards beyond a small plantation, shortly after passing which we cut across country to Drizzlecombe. And what hard work we made of that, with heathery scrub and clitter, we could not have chosen a rougher route. Once on the plain it was easier going and we were soon at the start of our unknown valley, where we found a good path to follow on the hill slopes a little above the river. We knew nothing of leats and tracks in those days and since the hillside contains some of each there is no doubt that we were following one or other of them. I do not remember having any difficulty crossing Evil Combe, though it can be unpleasantly wet here, and we were quite oblivious of the prominent mining remains at Crane Lake, except for the well-worn track there which we followed for some way beyond the combe before turning up the hill towards Nun's Cross, which was our ultimate objective.

Though the name was very familiar to me I do not think that I had revisited it since my boyhood days, when of course the farm was occupied and I remember being given a glass of milk here. Now it was deserted, the windows boarded up, and the original cottage beside it, once picturesquely roofed with thatch but now by ugly corrugated iron, falling into ruin. Fortunately I took a photograph of it then, for now alas it is only rubble.

From here we climbed the rising ground southerly to reach two cairns on the summit of Eylesbarrow Hill. A good path led us there, but it was rough going on the far side until we reached the mine track to lead us back to Burracombe Gate. When I look back now I marvel that we were so unaware of the extensive remains of the mining activity here. But knowing nothing of the presence of a mine and having no interest in the subject then, the numerous mounds and pits were just part of the Dartmoor scenery and did not seem remarkable. Far more to the point was that we had achieved a splendid walk through largely unknown country, on a perfect day, and had enjoyed the novelty then of each others company and comradeship.

Yes Tor

A more ambitious walk of this early period was one made possible by the availability of two cars. This enables one to plan a cross country walk instead of the more usual 'there and back' or circular one. Several such were to follow. In this particular case we took to the Okehampton road and parked one of the cars by the roadside a mile or so beyond the village of Sourton. In the other car we drove to the military road beyond Okehampton Camp, our destination being the base of Rough Tor, which at that time I pronounced Ruff Tor, not realising that it should rhyme with cow. The plan was to climb this tor, then the following West Mill Tor, and beyond that again, Yes Tor.

So off we went, up and up and up, a long steady climb. After passing the first tor it seemed such a long way to the next that I was under the impression that we had arrived at Yes Tor, only to find another huge tor looming ahead, and still some way off. On we plodded and eventually reached our objective, where we sat and rested and enjoyed our breakfast. Splendid views extended east and north and west, but to the south only a short stretch of level moorland leading to High Willes. Where the Ordnance Survey found the name High Willhays I do not know, it certainly should not be pronounced like that, and Crossing spells it Willes. The rock formation here is insignificant and therefore does not warrant it being classed as a tor, though at 2039 feet we were now on the highest point on Dartmoor. The view south now was breathtaking, in the crystal clear atmosphere all the details stood out sharply, though I was not at this stage sufficiently familiar with the northern moor to recognise them all.

Having drunk our fill we made the very steep and long descent westwards to the West Okement River. About half way down Bernard did the first of his celebrated tumbles. He tripped over something and just let himself go, a theory he had that if you did just that you would never hurt yourself. After rolling over he came gently to rest, unhurt but quite willing to rest awhile and recover. I say 'celebrated' for in subsequent

1. Bernard approaching the summit rocks of Fur Tor.

2. 1,877 feet up.

3. The view looking north from Fur Tor.

4. Tavy Cleave, my grandchildren bathing. This lovely setting has now lost its trees, washed away in the flood of December 1979.

5. Wallabrook clapper.

6. Teignhead Farm, 1967.

7. Grey Wethers.

8. Cranmere Pool, July 1967.

years he always seemed to manage to have one such fall during our series of walks. Nowadays, in our family, if anyone has a tumble it is always referred to as 'doing a Bernard'.

I cannot remember our actual route to the river or where we crossed it. I think it must have been to the north of Black Tor Copse, which I certainly do not remember seeing, and on the far side of the river we only followed the valley for a short distance before climbing out of it. I never had any apprehensions about crossing rivers, there always seemed to be boulders somewhere suitably spaced enabling one to leap across, and in those days I was more sure of my footing and balance than I am now. I am sure we had no difficulty on this occasion.

Our route then was to skirt the lower slopes of Corn Ridge, across the divide between that hill and the Sourton Tors, then via Prewley Moor and under the railway arch to the road not far from our parked car.

We postponed the retrieving of the second car until the afternoon when we returned to the northern moors with a picnic tea and were able to show Nancy the scene of part of our adventure and other areas of the Moor she had not seen before.

Fur Tor

In comparison with Yes Tor and High Willes as the highest points on Dartmoor, Fur Tor and its neighbour Cut Hill, in my opinion, are the most remote and difficult of access, being just about in the centre of the northern moors and surrounded for the most part by difficult terrain. Their heights are 1877 feet and 1968 feet respectively. I still cannot appreciate these heights in metres, it doesn't mean the same to me.

Bernard and I undertook this walk on 10th July 1967. The date I can be sure of because, although I was not keeping a diary of my walks as I do now, I took some coloured slides and dated them. By this time I was sufficiently knowledgeable and confident to have no doubt about finding my way, but being new ground I was not sure what hazards to expect. Beginners luck I suppose, for we experienced none, though on all subsequent occasions some difficulty or other has occurred, which I think may best be related now.

Years later my brother Dennis and I, during what I call the walking season, (I don't attempt much in the winter) used to meet about once a week for a walk. He had never been to Fur Tor so this was chosen for one of these occasions. All my walks to Fur Tor have started at Bagga Tor, where the lane from Peter Tavy ends just beyond Wapsworthy. We reached the River Tavy at a point approximately where Fur Tor Brook joins the river and decided to have our lunch there prior to attempting the climb to the Tor. Before we had finished that welcome break fog descended upon us. Obviously the attempt had to be abandoned, so we set off for home, climbing out of the valley and starting off in what I thought was the right direction. Soon after, to my surprise, we came to a valley on our left. "There shouldn't be a valley there" I said, and decided it was about time I used my compass. We had walked in a semi-circle and were back at the valley we had so recently left. I had read stories of people going round in circles in fogs on Dartmoor but never thought it would happen to me. It made me realise how important it was always to make use of the compass under these conditions, and from then on we made constant checks on it. Luckily we had no more difficulties, the remarkable thing about it being that we were on reasonably good ground all the way to Lynch Tor, the rising ground on our left letting me know that we had arrived there. We came out of the fog as we descended towards Bagga Tor, what a welcome relief it was.

Some years later, August 5th 1981, we made a second attempt for Fur Tor, but this time decided we would follow the old peat track, shown on the map as leading approximately in the right direction. That should provide us with a reasonably good path for most of the way, I thought. After some time the top of a tor appeared over the skyline ahead. "There's Fur Tor", I said, but on closer inspection decided it didn't look like Fur Tor and it seemed still an awful long way off. Better consult the compass. Good God, that tor is due north of us, we ought to be walking east. And 'that tor' proved to be Great Links Tor, we were way off our route and had to make the appropriate change of direction. I was really punished for my mistake, for we ran into some very bad ground, wet, hummocky, tufty long grass, very very tiring stuff. My ego suffered as much as my legs. What sort of a guide was I to make such a mistake? I'm really feeling exhausted. I'm a fool to be going on, I should turn round and go home. But Dennis had gone on ahead and wearily I plodded on until eventually we reached the river, in much the same place as on our previous adventure here. We sat and rested by the river bank, had our lunch as before and recovered our spirits. "I am not climbing Fur Tor today" I said, and shuddered at the thought of returning over that awful ground again. "Let's go back by the river". And this we decided to do, with the result that my body and mind returned to normal and this part of the walk was thoroughly enjoyable. One of the most satisfying places on the river, scenically, I think is where it makes its turn west and Amicombe Brook joins it, Sandy Ford. One of many Sandy Fords. All have their charm, but none so fine as this one, with the great hills around it and valleys leading to their mysterious sources. Then the cleave between the Meads and Watern Oke, good going beside the river bank until approaching Rattlebrook's entrance on the scene, where the hill descends so steeply it is quite a scramble to negotiate it. Tavy Cleave is always a thrill. This was the first time though that I had followed its left bank. We were getting so much pleasure from it that we continued for too long and we found ourselves confronted by the walls of Standon Farm.

Once again we were punished for a mistake. The climb beside the enclosures was steep and rocky. When we did reach the plain, tall bracken covered the ground. What we did not realise was that the bracken hid a rock field. This is most dangerous ground, for a fall in here and an injury and no one would find you. It was torture after our long walk, and there was a lot of it. Even after we were clear of that, and we had reached the Farm and its drive leading over Baggator Brook, we still had that steep stony lane, part of the Lych Way, to get back to our car. Never before or since have I said at the end of a walk, "Thank God that's over".

Dennis never did get to Fur Tor.

I made another attempt to reach the Tor, on my own this time, in the hot summer and drought of 1976. I got as far as the Peat Pass near Walkham Head, but the heat was too exhausting, with unbroken sunshine, to attempt to go further. But on a later occasion, when my son-in-law David Bruce was able to accompany me, we chose this same route, the object being to explore new ground higher up the Tavy, crossing it at Tavy Hole where two little feeders enter the river, and then across Fur Tor Brook near its head. We found new ground alright, a bit of Dartmoor's notorious fen, broken up by fissured peat. But there was not too much of it and we soon approached the Tor on comparatively level ground. It always disappoints me to find other people at these remote places, but such is the popularity of Dartmoor now that it has to be expected. It is just as disappointing to find the litter left there by some of them.

We returned via the river but left it earlier than on the previous occasion, climbing up by the two lateral streams in the Cleave when Ger Tor comes in sight. Then through the settlement of hut circles and so to Standon Farm. Weary, but not played out as before.

After these varied experiences it will be a bit of an anticlimax now to recount the walk in which everything went right. But it was a more testing walk than any Bernard and I had attempted so far, and if everything did go right we still experienced some bad ground, almost inevitable in this country. We were younger and fitter then so it did not worry us. We were blessed with perfect weather again and the view of the northern moors when we eventually reached our destination is still impressed upon my memory. (Plate 3)

We found the letter box and duly signed the visitor's book. What happens to these old books, does anyone ever look at them again? Then whilst I was doing something else I suddenly realised that Bernard had climbed to the very top of the tor rocks. That I had to have a picture of (Plate 2). Not to be outdone I climbed up beside him, an experience I am glad to have accomplished. But coming down I found much more difficult for one cannot see where to put one's foot. How do these rock-climbers do it? In one place I just had to let myself go to drop, only a foot or so, onto a ledge I knew was there but could not see. I felt most apprehensive about that.

Cut Hill looked invitingly close and such was my physical fitness then that I am quite sure it could have been included in the walk. But Bernard turned down my suggestion, which I have always regretted, for I have never since made any attempt to go there.

The homeward journey was uneventful and as I have so often found, did not seem so far as the outward one. But what satisfaction it gave us, and I have some splendid colour slides to give a perpetual reminder of that day.

Teignhead Farm

Two days after that walk (more colour slides confirm the date as 12th July 1967) we planned another long walk involving two cars. The first we left at the Warren House Inn; the second at Batworthy Corner, near Kes Tor.

The first items of interest were the stone rows and the menhir known as the Longstone, which we spent some time examining and photographing. Then followed the long and not very interesting trudge beside the boundary wall of Fernworthy Plantation. The dismal depths of these closely packed trees I find depressing. There are forest walks amongst them and interesting antiquities such as stone rows, stone circles and fine examples of hut circles to be found in the clearings, many of which I have still not seen and have little desire to look for in such surroundings, where they are quite out of their element.

Our objective was the clapper bridge across the North Teign River which gave access to Teignhead Farm. I have since found much more interesting ways of getting there, though the route we took is perhaps the shortest. The way I would recommend now and which I have chosen on several occasions, is to walk due west from Batworthy Corner to Stonetor Bottom, near where Stonetor Brook flows into the Teign. This way one can enjoy the wonderful panoramic views of the Teign basin and its surrounding hills and tors. There are some unpleasant mires in the basin but if one keeps to the direct line described the ground will be found firm and dry. Then follow the river up through its most exciting section, Manga Hole, where the river forms a waterslide over massive bedrock in which the water has worn numerous hollows. I regret that Bernard never saw this unforgettable bit of Dartmoor scenery. Above the falls, if they can be called such, and not far from the right bank, may be found the ruinous remains of a blowing-house and the leat which brought water to it.

But to return to the route we had taken, when we reached the end of the plantation a gate in the transverse wall led to a track descending to the bridge. The panorama of the western hills was spread out before us, a group of trees in the foreground showing us where the old farm lay. We descended to the bridge and there we sat for a while, pondering on the making of it, and the sort of life a moorman lived in this lonely place.

Eric Hemery in "High Dartmoor" tells us something about it and a fascinating story it makes, beginning with the first occupier of the farm, one William Rogers, who in 1780, when making this bridge, sledged the massive granite slabs down Manga Hill over the frozen ground. With the primitive tools and facilities available at that time it seems an incredible feat.

We walked up to the farm which we found to be in reasonably sound condition with a good slate roof. My photograph of it shows it pleasantly surrounded by trees, a slot-bar gate-post at the entrance to the court (Plate 6). There was a notice pinned to one of the trees which said PRIVATE. TRESPASSING FORBIDDEN. So we did not make a closer inspection of it. I wish we had, for when some years later I visited it again I was saddened to find nothing but a heap of rubble where the house had been. In the 1966 edition of Crossing's "Dartmoor Worker" there is a photograph of it taken by Robert Burnard in 1889 when it had a thatched roof, primitive but picturesque. Hemery shows it as it was in 1952, with gaping holes for windows and its porch derelict. Its restored state as we found it in 1967 was, I believe, the work of the military. By whom, then, and when, was it so completely demolished? The oasis of trees now guards its grave. Let us hope the splendid clapper bridge does not suffer the same fate.

We retraced our steps to the bridge and beyond it turned right to the little valley that leads up to the Grey Wethers Stone Circles, which neither of us had seen before. We were duly impressed, not knowing then that they had been extensively restored, at about the turn of the century, under the direction of the Rev. Sabine Baring-Gould, the heavy work being performed by George French of Postbridge, who organised the carting of twenty-six loads of stone to help trig up the fallen stones, many of which had lain buried beneath the turf. Their diameters are

116 feet and 103 feet and have the distinction of being the largest on Dartmoor. Nowhere else are there two such circles so close together (Plate 7).

The last part of our walk was a long slog, across the wet ground forming the source of the South Teign River, then over Whit Ridge to the head of Stannon Brook, where we looked for a stone row shown on the map as being near to the newtake wall. Not surprisingly we did not find it. If ever there had been one here it does not exist now. However Worth's "Dartmoor" mentions (page 225) a double one a little to the NNW of that marked by OS, which I have since found, and on the occasion of a walk with the Devon Archaeological Society led by Tom Greeves we followed the whole length of this row, over 600 feet long, into Stannon Newtake to a small terminal stone and nearby cairn. Apart from a few prominent but small stones at the higher end of the row, all the stones are small, most only just visible above ground level, others no doubt remain buried. At the high end a circular patch of flat ground marks the site of a cairn and beyond it a fairly large recumbent stone may or may not have been associated with the row.

Having given up our hunt for the missing row we plodded on to Watern Hill, the afternoon was getting hot and so were we, thankful at last to reach the Warren House Inn where we indulged in the most welcome pint of beer I can ever remember drinking.

We still had to retrieve the car at Batworthy Corner of course and then return unsociably in our respective cars to Tavistock. That was the least enjoyable part of the day, when we could have done with each others company to overcome a desire to fall asleep at the wheel.

* * * * * *

Bernard and I had many more walks together of course, equally enjoyable, but none stand out in my memory so much as those described, perhaps because we were discovering new ground, but also I am sure because the weather in every case could not have been more perfect, when Dartmoor looked its loveliest. Such walks took us to many and varied parts of the Moor. To Cranmere Pool (Plate 8), by the short route from Okement Hill, but we did include the more impressive peat pass on Black Ridge. To Duck's Pool, via the Langcombe Valley and Broad Rock, from which vantage point the head of the Erme Valley excited my imagination as somewhere to explore in the future. As a variation from the open moor we walked the length of the Dart Gorge from Dartmeet to Holne New Bridge. The beautiful Lustleigh Cleave and the Teign valley from Chagford to Fingle Bridge. And many more. They ended in the summer of 1984, when to mark the occasion Bernard once again demonstrated his ability to fall without hurting himself. At the age of 82 one cannot do that without the risk of a broken bone and I felt rather concerned for him. However he was alright and we continued to have our daily walks throughout his visit, the last being in the lovely Swincombe valley exploring the leats and remains of Gobbet Mine etc. He showed some signs of distress on hills but otherwise was his usual cheerful self. I was surprised and saddened therefore to hear of his death early in the following year.

Overlapping with the walks with Bernard were another series with my brother Dennis. He and I had seen little of each other since our school days. My work with Cable and Wireless took me to many stations abroad and finally to their Training School at Porthcurno in Cornwall. Dennis went out to Australia on the vineyards north of Adelaide, and on his return to England got married and settled in Exeter. Not until some time after we had both retired did the opportunity arise for regular meetings, resulting in the development of a close bond of fraternal affection and mutual interest in the exploration of Dartmoor.

Dennis's knowledge of the moor had been restricted mainly to its eastern side, apart from that of our childhood days and his camping with the scouts on a site in the Avon Valley, now, to his subsequent astonishment, submerged beneath the waters of the reservoir there. So he would rely on me to choose the venue for our walks and for the guiding of them. I was rather conscious of the fact that he had much the longer journey to make to our meeting place and thus it came about that a number of our walks commenced in the Chagford, Belstone and Okehampton areas, and I got to know that part of the Moor better than I might otherwise have done.

On one such walk which commenced at Belstone my grand-daughter Hilary, then aged about eighteen, came with us. To fall in with my advice about footwear she wore her wellington boots, but I did not realise that she only had thin silk stockings on inside them. The walk was a long one taking us over the Belstone Tors, Higher Tor, Winter Tor, Oke Tor, Hound Tor, Little Hound Tor, Small Brook and the River Taw back to Belstone. When I asked Hilary how she had enjoyed the walk she said "The first part was most enjoyable, the middle part bearable, the last part agony". The boots had given her blisters and she must have suffered, but I am proud of her fortitude in not once complaining.

My other grand-daughter, Joanna, also accompanied us on several occasions. She was a good walker and I used to call her 'sharpeyes' because she would often see things that I missed. My complaint now is their lack of consideration for their grandfather. Just as I was beginning to enjoy their company and looking forward to more of it, one of them has to go and get married and the other beetles off to France in pursuit of her career as a flautist.

Of the many walks we undertook in the Chagford area none I think is more memorable than that which semi-circled the huge bowl of the North Teign country across which that river and the Wallabrook snake their way before eventually joining at its eastern periphery. It took us over the high ground which encloses it, and thus it was in view nearly all the way, slightly hazed with the heat of the day.

Scorhill to Wild Tor, Teignhead Farm, Teign and Wallabrook

We met at the top of the lane which winds steeply and tortuously up its long length from Chagford Bridge, past Gidleigh and Berrydown to open out at Gidleigh Common.

Our first objective was the stone circle west of Buttern Hill, which was not easy to find as there is little of it left standing. A short distance to the north of it is the deep and narrow valley which Crossing says bears the name of Pixies' Parlour. We felt compelled to make a little detour to look into it and pay our respects to the little men.

From here our route took us to Rival Tor, otherwise known as Rippator or Ripper Tor, of no great height or mass. The ground falls away gently westward to Gallaven Brook, which has been extensively streamed for tin and where there is recorded to be a tinner's cache. We looked for that on another occasion but without success, that day also being memorable for being caught in a prolonged rain storm, which persuaded us to abandon the walk, and thinking to make a shorter route home, got into the mire below Rival Tor. You might say that expedition was a bit of a flop. But not so today, when we were blessed with perfect weather, though by the time we had completed the long uphill slog to Wild Tor we were hot and sticky and only too glad to sit for awhile and enjoy the view. At 1730 feet that was the high point of our walk, though Watern Tor, our next objective, is not far below it. The lamellar rock formation on this tor is striking.

From here we made for the corner of the great newtake wall of Teignhead Farm. The enclosing of such a vast area of land caused great consternation to the Gidleigh commoners when it was built. The labour involved in its construction is in keeping with the sledging of the stones for the clapper bridge. A convenient gate near the corner enabled us to enter the enclosure and descend to Hew Lake where we had our lunch by the little stream.

Suitably rested and refreshed we continued on our way to Teignhead Farm. This was the occasion when I was so surprised to find the old homestead in ruins. How has it come about that it is so completely razed? Nearby Manga House, of greater age than Teignhead Farm for it was abandoned before the latter was built, has far more of its old walls still standing.

Our walk continued beyond the farm towards Varracombe Brook, but a heavy menacing black cloud in that direction dissuaded us from going further in that direction, though as it turned out it amounted to nothing. We did, however, discover by chance the blowing-house nearby with its unusual mould-stone and the broken piece of another in the wall near the river. Since it was not marked on the map it was quite an exciting find.

We kept to the left bank of the Teign on our return journey, descending through Manga Hole. After crossing Hew Lake (which name apparently is a corruption of Wood Lake, and the place where we had partaken of our lunch is known as Wood Hole) and passing through a hunting-gate in the newtake wall we took Crossing's advice on page 240 of his 'Guide' and left the river at this point to skirt a swampy area, and steered northward over good ground to the Wallabrook. Crossing mentions a small shepherd's hut on this section (Will May's House according to Hemery) which we looked for in vain. The Wallabrook was then our companion as far as the single clapper bridge across it (Plate 5). And so up to the famous Scorhill Circle and to our starting point.

* * * * * *

William Crossing in an appendix to his book "One Hundred Years on Dartmoor", lists practically all the tors on Dartmoor and their location. When I obtained my copy of this book I made a practice of entering the date beside the name of the tor as I succeeded in visiting it. Thus I know that the two walks just described took place on 23 August 1978 and 13 September 1978 respectively. Quite a number of other tors in various parts of the moor are dated 1978. It must have been a fine summer and I certainly seem to have taken advantage of it. Green Tor bears the date 30.8.78. As I have only once visited this tor it must be the day Dennis and I planned the walk from . . .

Okehampton to Lydford

This of course meant leaving one car at Lydford (by the roadside near the Dartmoor Inn) and the other at Okehampton near the Military Camp.

The track beside Moor Brook was followed to Black Down and thence to the ford across Red-a-ven Brook. The slopes of Yes Tor rose high on our left and fell to the interesting looking steep sided valley between Longstone Hill and Homerdon Hill, unnamed on the map but which

Crossing names Fishcombe and the stream Fishcombe Water. Some rather wet ground followed as we approached Black Tor, whose rocks we visited and looked down into the valley of the West Okement and Black Tor Copse.

A gradual and pleasant descent brought us finally to the river near Sandy Ford, with Lints Tor standing out boldly above us like a medieval castle. We had visited this tor earlier in the year with Joanna as companion. Lints Tor Brook descends beside it. After crossing it we kept close to the main river, my recollection of this section being one of particular pleasure. Such a place to me is Dartmoor at its most thrilling. The steep of Amicombe Hill on one side, the slopes of Lints Tor on the other, Great Kneeset ahead with a little valley beside it, the river tracing the depths of these lofty hills and providing us with a musical divertimento. No other human beings or animals in sight, we are alone in the world and all around us is ours for the moment. What a bountiful gift of Nature to provide such luxury as a setting for our luncheon.

Our next problem was to find a crossing place over the river. Having found it a patch of mire on the far side provided another hazard. The only way to cross it was to make a hurried dash for the far side before our feet sank into it. Luckily we succeeded without getting our feet wet, though I must confess that my heart was beating a good bit faster for awhile afterwards. Thus does Dartmoor offer you blessings with one hand and perils with the other, and so we learn to respect it.

Good ground now allowed us to make good progress towards the nameless little tributary that descends to the west of Great Kneeset. This valley, Broad Amicombe Hole, enabled a fairly gentle ascent to be made to the heights of Amicombe Hill, which we now had to cross for our route to Lydford. It was rather rough going for most of the way to Green Tor, bleak and uninteresting after the scenery we had so recently enjoyed. No wonder the ruins of the house beneath the tor is called Bleak House, though its setting beside the Rattlebrook is a deal more picturesque than the open moor over which we had laboured.

More rough ground followed beneath the Dunnagoat Tors, for somehow we missed a good path here which would have taken us to the Rattlebrook Mine track. We did locate the track eventually near the col between Great Links Tor and Chat Tor. Then followed that spectacular bit of scenery at Dick's Well where Doe Tor Brook is born and where the tinners of old had lowered the level of the ground over a vast area and dug those incredibly deep gerts.

At the next col, between Arms Tor and Brai Tor, we were in sight of our destination, Lydford, and a view beyond it to Cornwall. There followed the long familiar descent to High Down Ford, and as we crossed by the stepping stones I was reminded of my first visit here, so many years ago now, when, one early morning, I had it all to myself and thought what a delightfully peaceful place it was. Only sometime later did I realise that it was a very popular picnic spot, when the hillside is dotted with the ubiquitous motor car, even down to the river side. And that is how it looked this day, a somewhat jarring note after the loneliness of our walk, which we rated as one of our most successful and enjoyable.

* * * * * * *

I am quite well aware that these "rambles", as Crossing would call them, would not be classed as long to those intrepid walkers who undertake the "Ten Tors" or the full "Abbots' Way" walks, and even quite paltry to those gluttons for punishment who enter for the "Dartmoor 100". But these walks are more in the nature of competitions, a test of endurance and navigation. As such I can appreciate the satisfaction of being first home or even of completing the marathon. How many of those walkers though want to go back to Dartmoor because it is Dartmoor? Its unique qualities surely cannot be appreciated under such conditions. One's age I suppose has something to do with it. When young one needs the challenge of a race or proof of one's physical fitness. With advancing years one cannot hope to compete in such adventures, so one accepts Dartmoor as a challenge in itself. Spring has gone from one's step and autumn is in one's bones. You can no longer leap across a stream but wobble shakily from boulder to boulder and hope your balance does not let you down. Slow speed and frequent pauses are necessary when climbing the steep hills, but then there is time to look around and enjoy the view whilst you recover. The challenge is still there and the satisfaction is just as great when the difficulties and distances are overcome. But you learn to love Dartmoor for what it is, always somethhing to find, a new place, a new view, another piece of the jig-saw puzzle that makes up its varied history.

So the next two walks to be described are just as much an achievement for me as the successful completion of any of the above great walks must be to their participants.

The Abbots' Way

Eric Hemery suggests that the marked route on the Ordnance Survey maps is not the true route which the monks would have taken across the Moor from Buckfast to Buckland or Tavistock. More correctly this is the Jobbers' Path, which the wool merchants would have used. The monks marked their path with a series of primitive granite crosses, which still survive, across Down Ridge, Ter Hill, skirting Fox Tor Mire to Siward's Cross, Newlycombe Cross, Crazywell Cross and others beyond. That of course is reasonable and convincing, but the Abbots' Way Walk is now so well-established that even if the Ordnance Survey amended their maps, the present route is still likely to be the chosen one, it is much more rugged and offers a greater challenge.

The full walk from Buckfast to Tavistock is about 26 miles, only a portion of which is over the open moor. And only a part of that, some ten miles, constitutes the walk now to be described, but those ten miles cover the most remote and exciting part of it.

Dennis's son David, who has the distinction of going on the first ever Ten Tors Walk, accompanied us on this occasion. We met at Cross Furzes, leaving one car there and driving the other to Princetown and Castle Road to Whiteworks, where our walk commenced.

Whiteworks has been the start or finish of many of my walks, a very early one being with Bernard when we made a circular tour of the notorious Fox Tor Mire. I met with a minor accident on that occasion, slipping on a small boulder as we crossed Nun's Cross Brook, getting a wellington-boot full of water and mildly straining my wrist as I put my hand out to save myself from further immersion. I thought little of it at the time but I have had a weakness in my right wrist ever since.

Here also has been the scene of many days exploration of Whiteworks Tin Mine, the tracing of its leats, the finding of its shafts, adits, wheelpits, tramway and whim-plats. The hunting for other mining, historic and prehistoric remains. And more recently a walk with the Dartmoor Preservation Association, led by Tom Greeves, who pointed out to us the area of land around the confluence of the Swincombe and Strane Rivers, near where the dam would have been built had the Swincombe Reservoir ever materialised, which had just then been bought by the DPA as a result of a legacy left for this purpose by Miss M.L.Trahair.

Our walk on this day, however, took us away from this scene, along the old cart track that leads to Nun's Cross Farm. The Abbots' Way, whichever of the two routes is considered to be the correct one, would have passed over this col, the venerable Siward's Cross marking the way. A ford on the Nun's Cross Brook is a likely part of this route, a well-defined track leading to and away from it. Its continuation eastwards may be correct for the Ter Hill/Down Ridge route, but not for the direction we needed to go for Plym Ford. The OS map shows a curious dog-leg route between the two places, but no path has ever existed to warrant such a marking, so one has to make one's own choice of ground and direction over the hill to get there.

Plym Ford itself is perhaps not the ideal place to cross the river, unless one is prepared to wade across, though ideal no doubt for the Jobbers' ponies. But the river has not as yet attained any great size and easy crossing places are to be found either side of it. We followed the map route from here, a gentle climb around Great Gnats Head, cresting the bowl of Dead Man's Bottom to Broad Rock. We were unanimous in agreeing later that this was the least enjoyable part of the walk. It seemed endless and arduous over long withered grass with little in the way of views to relieve it. And we did not find Broad Rock, which lies hidden in a hollow if one passes to the north of it. Once we had reached the crest of the hill and the broad expanse of Erme Head came in sight, the view that had so excited me on that walk with Bernard to Duck's Pool, all was changed.

Now we had something to interest us all the time. First to keep clear of the miry head of the river, then the astonishing depths of Erme Pits where the ancient tinners had laboured. The first crossing of the infant river, followed by an easy walk along its left bank to the ford on its first tributary, the Wollake, which seemed to be contributing more water than the principal river. Then followed Dry Lake and beyond it a siting of the stones of the longest stone row on the Moor, its origin being nearly two miles to the south on Stall Moor. Red Lake, and red it really was; we crossed well below the fording place shown on the map, with the result that we climbed Brown Heath some way south of the true route and met the Redlake railway track near the filter beds associated with the old china clay works, for which mistake of navigation I was not at all displeased, for otherwise we should have missed these interesting remains. We spent some time examining them and wondered how water could possibly have been conducted to them. Also from this vantage point we had a splendid view of the Erme Valley and the huge loop the railway had to take along the contour of Quickbeam Hill. The terminus of the railway is the conspicuous conical mound of china clay waste which had been in view to the north as we crossed Red Lake.

We must have regained the Abbots' Way near Crossways but found nothing to indicate a track, so made our own way over the top of the hill, now to expose an entirely new section of the Moor, the Avon Valley, the river descending from its treacherous source mire way out on our left and turning sharply eastwards below us to flow between Huntingdon's Heap of Sinners and the Eastern and Western White Barrows. Our destination was almost in view but still a long way off.

We descended to the clapper bridge, not an ancient one but built by the warrener of Huntingdon Warren sometime during the nineteenth century. We were deviating from the true route of course, but it is a much more convenient way to cross the river and it leads to a pleasant path parallel with the river's left bank all the way to the Western Wellabrook, where stands the only cross on this route, Huntingdon Cross. I told David the story of Keble Martin's chapel, and the presence nearby of a large wheel-pit associated with Huntingdon Mine. He was interested enough and had plenty of energy left to walk up the Western Wellabrook to find these items for himself, whilst Dennis and I rested our weary bones until his return.

From here the path is very well defined and ere long the Avon Reservoir came into view, and soon after Brockhill Water. The foot of this little stream is now lost beneath the waters of the reservoir, though I did see it on a later occasion (1984) when a severe drought lowered the level of the water to expose it, together with an interesting old blowing-house which I had never expected to have the opportunity of seeing. Also on that occasion we had noticed that the water in the river above the reservoir was curiously discoloured. Not until Broadafalls was reached was the reason for this apparent. A blue plastic pipeline was observed trailing up the valley of Heng Lake. It was now obvious that water was being pumped or siphoned from the lake that now fills the china clay pit to augment the waters of the Avon.

The weary ascent of Grippers Hill was rather an anticlimax after what had gone before, it seemed longer than it really was to Water Oke Corner, with nothing to see but rising ground ahead. Then the crest was reached and the view of the in-country's green fields confirmed that our journey was nearly over. An easy descent over Lambs Down to the lovely wooded valley of the Dean Burn, across its dappled waters and up the stony steep lane, and there was the welcome sight of our car waiting to take us back to Whiteworks.

Black Lane

The first part of this walk from Whiteworks to Plym Ford covered the same ground as the previous one. But from Plym Ford we made a direct line to Great Gnats Head, looking for and finding a ruined kistvaen on the way. Only two side stones and one end stone which had fallen in, remain.

We did not linger at Great Gnats Head for a cloud of flies made the visit unpleasant. Rather rough ground followed to Erme Head and this time we kept to the north side of the mire and found good going as far as Wollake, which tributary we now followed, soon crossing to the left bank and making for a conspicuous pile of boulders which we suspected might hide Phillpotts' Cave, and were pleased to find that they did so.

The path which now revealed itself above the left bank of the brook we hoped might be the Blacklane Path, it was certainly going in the right direction. Soon the sight of a tall wooden post ahead gave us the encouragement we needed, for surely it could not mark anything else. After passing the post the path veered to the east, which was not the direction we wanted to go. Straight ahead was a mire-bounded feeder of the Blacklane Brook. What should we do? There seemed to be firm ground on the far side, not all that far away. I did not fancy taking what may be a long detour. Let's make a dash for it. It proved an unpleasant experience and we deservedly got our boots filled with black slime and had to endure wet feet from then on, though the discomfort did not last long. We soon picked up the path again on the far side. It was fairly obvious now that the path had deviated around the source of this mire and that we should have followed it.

Parts of this walk so far described have previously been mentioned. They will appear again in further walks. Inevitable I suppose since it is country that has given me so much pleasure. The only reason for including this day's outing in the series of nostalgic walks is because of the section we were about to traverse, which will definitely not be repeated.

The term 'waste' on Dartmoor refers to areas of common land small in size and of rough pasture, but only found on the southern part of the Moor adjacent to the in-country. New Waste, Highhouse Waste, Dendles Waste etc. You will find them marked on the map. My dictionary gives its meaning, when referring to land, as 'desert, dreary scene or expanse, uninhabited, desolate, barren, monotonous, without features of interest'. That describes exactly what we now saw ahead of us. A leaden grey sky roofed a large flat bowl, no view of rolling hills, no rocks, no river, no wildlife, just gently rising ground in all directions except that from which we had come, enclosing an area of mire and scrub. A depression in the land. A depression on the mind. Yet it was what I had come to see. I wanted the experience of this mood of the Moor. I can think of no other place on Dartmoor that can give such a sense of loneliness, remoteness, apprehension. What if fog descended on us now? What if we got caught in heavy rain or a thunderstorm? What if we got stugged in the mire? It could be days or weeks before anyone came this way again. I drank my fill of these feelings as I looked around me, for I knew I would not come here again. I had seen it, experienced it, that was enough. We trudged on, thankful for the path and relieved when we saw another wooden post in the distance, and knew that we were heading in the right direction. When we reached it we found the words 'Caters Beam' inscribed on it. I had been there before and had looked into this bowl from the opposite direction and thought, I must walk there one day.

I knew the ground ahead now. Fox Tor came into view. All would be well. But I shall never forget that scene of desolation.

DPA Walk, Yealm Head, Erme Head

The walks with Dennis came to an end when he decided to move to Nottingham. I have always been well-content to walk on my own and in fact considered that one discovered more that way, for one is not distracted by conversation. With advancing age however I began to feel the need of companionship and decided to join the Dartmoor Preservation Association's guided walks, of which there are some five or six a year. Thus I made new acquaintances and friends, many more knowledgeable of the Moor than I, and so I added to my store of knowledge. Increasingly though it became difficult to keep up with the group and I found myself tail-end-Charlie on many occasions. This culminated in a walk which I was looking forward to with relish but wondered whether I could tackle it. The plan was to start from New Waste Moorgate, near Cornwood, follow the Yealm Valley to the source of its river, walk along the top of that long long ridge which extends from Shell Top to Great Gnats Head, visit Ducks Pool, descend Wollake to the Erme, join the two-mile long stone row to the Dancers, thence via Staldon Row back to New Waste.

Much of this route I was familiar with but not the upper reaches of the Yealm and that long long ridge. That was what I wanted to experience.

All went well to begin with. At Yealm Steps we examined the upper blowing-house and we had our picnic lunch at Yealm Head beside a Blachford boundary stone. The weather was fine, walking conditions good if rough in places. I had kept up with the group and I was feeling well-satisfied with myself. When we resumed the walk however I found the last bit of climbing to the ridge rather laborious. I had to make frequent stops and my pace became slower and slower. By the time I reached level ground the group was out of sight, a long way ahead. Then near disaster struck. My left leg went down a hole up to my knee and of course I fell over. Having got myself into a sitting position I tried to extricate my leg but found I could not, the suction was too great. Here is a pretty kettle of fish I thought, stuck in the middle of nowhere and little chance of any help. Eventually, by clasping my hands together beneath my knee and pulling with all my strength I managed to get my leg free. No sooner had I got myself upright and commenced to walk than the whole performance was repeated, this time it was my right leg that went down a hole. Fortunately it was not so difficult to free it this

9. Stepping-stones have a great appeal for me, often to be found in beautiful surroundings. On the Sheepstor Brook at Colleytown.

10. On the River Dart at Swincombe Meet.

11. The idyllic setting of the Swincombe Meet stones.

12. The mingling of the waters. If ever there are places where spirits gather, this must be one of them. Langcombe Meet, a scene that never ceases to thrill me, beckoning me on into that long lonely valley, haunted with history, spellbound by scenery, bewitched by mystery, the names Dead Man's Bottom, Grim's Grave, only hinting at the stories they hide.

13. A fine example of staddles, so surprisingly complete, at the medieval farm known as Hook-in-the-Tor, near Long Ash, Merrivale.

14. David admiring the view from Lints Tor.

15. One of Dartmoor's gems. Doe Tor Falls.

16. High Down Ford and stepping-stones. We are returning from a walk via Doe Tor Brook and Rattlebrook to Kitty Tor.

17. John examines a small kistvaen south of Dead Man's Bottom. A larger one nearby we found to be so covered with vegetation it was hardly recognisable. The Dartmoor National Park were alerted to its condition. They have promised to effect some restoration.

18. John and David departing from a kistvaen on Calveslake Hill. Higher and Lower Hart Tors and a prehistoric pound on the far side of the Plym valley.

Photo; John Pegg

19. Majestic monarch of Drizzlecombe, that sanctuary surely of Celtic lords.

Photo; John Pegg

20. David and I congratulate each other on the successful ascent of Everest!

Photo; David Edgley

21. I point out to John the still well-marked leats which supplied the Redlake's reservoirs from this wilderness of wetness, north of the spoil-heap.

Photo; David Edgley

22. Redlake's flooded clay-pit. The sky is darkening to the west. By the time we had descended we were enveloped in fog (see page 37).

23. Members of the Dartmoor Preservation Association preparing for lunch at Yealm Head. BB stone marks the bounds of Blachford, Cornwood (see page 32).

time. Then I heard a voice call "Are you alright?" Two people, not of our group, were passing across the ridge to the south of me. They must have wondered what on earth I was doing performing such strange antics on the ground. I assured them that I was and continued on my way, but feeling not a little shaken. I chose my way carefully, but with no hope of catching up with the group I wondered how long it was going to take me to get home. Two more figures appeared, ahead now, and I was relieved to recognise Colin Kilvington and Cyril Phillips, they had come back to look for me. I was glad of the support of Colin's arm and we made better progress to Broad Rock, upon which I sat whilst Colin lifted each of my legs in turn and emptied out a stream of dirty brown water from my wellingtons. I was able to laugh at the whole episode now.

We decided to abandon the section of the walk to Duck's Pool and descend the Erme to Wollake and wait there for the main body of the group. It gave me some pleasure to be able to show my companions the A Head stone, which neither of them had found before. A good rest at Wollake Mill and a cup of hot coffee and I felt fully recovered, the rest of the walk passing without incident, though of course it was full of interest, particularly a kistvaen between Blachford Bottom and the Staldon stone row which I had not heard of let alone seen before. The sandy deposit in my wellingtons was beginning to cause some discomfort on the final stages of the walk and I was glad to have them removed, for I needed some assistance to get them off. My socks were in a sorry state. My pedometer indicated only five miles, what a joke. I have found that it does not register on soft ground and particularly I suppose if one's step is cushioned with a bootful of water!

This experience made me realise that I could no longer go on these long walks with the DPA, in spite of the welcome and consideration that I was always given. I was still capable of walking such distances but only at my own pace. Indeed a few weeks after this event I went for just such a long walk on my own.

Jobbers' Road

Eric Hemery's "Walking Dartmoor's Ancient Tracks" had just been published and I decided to follow the first part of his "Jobbers' Road", commencing from Burracombe Gate. The first section to Thrushelcombe Ford is clearly marked on the map of the "Ellisborough Mine". It crosses the mine track some quarter of a mile beyond Burracombe Gate and is marked by a boulder beside the track, unmistakeable because there are no other boulders in the vicinity. The track is particularly evident on the north side of the road and is in fact shown as a short black line on OS

Leisure Map. How easy is this route compared with that which Bernard and I had taken to Drizzlecombe over Whittenknowles Rocks!

From the ford on Thrushelcombe Hemery takes one on a rather circuitous route via the kistvaen and menhirs of the Drizzlecombe "sanctuary". I followed his instructions here but cannot believe that the old jobbers would have lost height and gone further than was really necessary to get to Plym Steps. There are so many paths along the side of the Plym valley to select from anyway. My own view is that their path, if they had a selected one, would be on higher ground approximately along the heavy contour line (350m), where I have found a path which takes one to the well-worn broad track descending to Plym Steps.

What a pity there are no stepping stones at Plym Steps now. It is not easy to cross at the ford, unless one is wearing wellington boots and the river is low. Otherwise it is necessary to go higher up the river where it narrows somewhat and there are suitable boulders in the river. On a subsequent visit (with David and John) we found that someone had placed a series of relatively small stones across the ford and with the aid of two walking sticks I managed to balance my way across dry-shod.

What a fascination they have, these old fords and steps. My photographs Plates 9, 10, 11, 16, show some fine examples. Not only do they link bank to bank, they link the present with the past. They conjure up a picture of pack-horse trains approaching in a long slow-moving file, the leading pony splashes and clatters his way across the ford, stops and lowers his head to drink of the cool clean water. The others follow and soon the river is filled with tired mudcovered animals all slaking their thirst, as I have seen cattle do here. One can visualise the tinners striding the stepping stones on their way to or from their labours; but can you see a monk gathering up his robes to leap the stones? No, I think not. He would ride sedately over the ford on mule or donkey, head bowed and making the sign of the cross.

From Plym Steps the route ascends Langcombe to Dead Man's Bottom, which is crossed at a ford higher up this little stream between two mires. I could find no track beyond the ford and took a compass bearing to Broad Rock. I had never before made any effort to find Erme Head Ford and Erme Pits Ford, but I had no difficulty in finding them and I was pleased to be able to cross at these historic places. At Wollake I left the Jobbers' Road and ascended that valley to that "parcel of land of about two acres in extent for which a rent of 3d was paid by Richard Coole and Thomas Hele, during the reign of King Henry VIII, and who there constructed an enclosure and building known as Wallack Mill". I identified and followed the watercourse which supplied the mill, as far as its miry source on Blacklane Brook, sometimes known as Dark Lake, though more correctly, according to Crossing, as Wollake.

And so to Duck's Pool, where I was relieved to find that the carcase of a dead cow whose putrefying body was, on a previous visit, polluting the atmosphere near the Memorial Stone, had completely disappeared.

This part of the country just described always thrills me, from Plym Steps, the Langcombe valley, Broad Rock, Erme Head and the high moor tributaries of Erme. Its remoteness, its links with the Moor's ancient activities, the tombs of prehistoric people, the labours of tin streaming, the stupendous task of digging out those huge pits, the long journeys of the tinners, the jobbers and the monks, if the last named ever did come this way. Where once was such a hive of activity and a recognised highway, where once was the sound of noisy machinery and the chatter of working men, where the newly dug earth left stark scars on the landscape, all is now silent and lonely, an incredible peace fills the land as well as body and mind. One needs to be on one's own fully to appreciate the atmosphere and associations of the place. That was how it was on this visit, how I felt, how I loved every moment of it.

Over the hill beyond Duck's Pool, into the Plym valley, crossing it above its head mire; the outlying workings of Wheal Katharine; the Ellisborough Mine track; and so to Burracombe Gate. Tired of course, but oh so refreshed in mind.

* * * * * * *

Soon after Bernard's death and Dennis's departure to Nottingham, and at the time when I was contemplating joining the DPA walks, some good fairy waved her magic wand, and lo!

I was returning from a shopping expedition in Tavistock, walking up the steep Green Hill to my home, when I was conscious of footsteps behind me. I turned to find a tall man obviously seeking a word with me. "You are John Robins are you not?" he asked. He then introduced himself as John Pegg and said he would like to present me with a copy of "A Visitors' Guide to Dartmoor" which he and his partner David Edgley had just produced. I was invited back to their cottage at the bottom of the hill. Thus began most valued friendships and another long series of walks, which surely was the answer to my wish for companionship on my ramblings.

Our first walk together was from Combestone Tor to Horn's Cross from where we traced a leat to Ringleshutts Mine, then re-traced it to its source on Hooten Wheals Stream. It was a blustery day in May 1985, with forecast of fog and rain. I was apprehensive in such conditions that I would be a drag on my new companions. I need not have worried.

They were kind and considerate, and so it has proved on all our subsequent walks, always keeping to my pace and never complaining.

It is not practical to recount the many walks that followed for so many of them covered routes already described, such as the Abbots' Way, though it is worth recalling that on the occasion when David and I did it we experienced almost continuous drizzle. Such conditions are testing but I am sure it strengthened the bond between us. I would like however to give an account of two expeditions that always give me a warm glow to recall.

Red Lake China Clay Works

We had, on one occasion, walked from Whiteworks to Red Lake China Clay Works, which was also my first visit there. Subsequently I read E.A.Wade's interesting book about this fascinating enterprise, and with this increased knowledge of it was desirous to go there again.

This time we started off from Cross Furzes and took the long lane past Hayford Hall to Lud Gate and then the track to Huntingdon Mine. Here I must break into this narrative to mention another walk, along the same route but which took place later, with Dave and Kathy Brewer. Kathy is an intrepid walker. We first met on my initial DPA walk. She it was who usually held back to keep me company when I lagged behind on these walks, a kindly gesture which was much appreciated. For health reasons Dave was rarely able to come, but I have corresponded with him frequently and exchanged much information, from which I was the major beneficiary. On the walk in question he was able to come too, the principle object of which was the examination of the Huntingdon Mine and the leats associated with it. I learned much that day, not the least of which was the astonishing extension of the leat from Broadafalls, originally cut for the Huntingdon Mine, to the River Mardle for Buckfastleigh Manor Copper Mine. At a later period in the Huntingdon Mine's existence a very large wheel-pit was constructed further down the valley and served by a deeply cut and impressive leat taken off the Western Wellabrook. The initial part of this leat still takes a major portion of the water from the river but after a short distance it is now returned to the main course of the stream. In the meantime the Buckfastleigh Manor Mine Company re-directed the course of the original leat from Broadafalls to allow it to enter the Wellabrook further down the river from its original crossing of it, and then extracting the water into the new cut to the Mardle. When the Huntingdon Mine cut their new leat they perforce had to launder the Buckfastleigh Mine leat over it, an intriguing feature which is well-worth looking for. Thus there is far more to be seen of this mine than I was aware of on this casual visit with John and David.

We could not have spent much time on examining the remains anyway, for the weather was unsettled and we felt it necessary to press on to our objective.

Skirting the enclosures of the warren house we climbed to the Heap of Sinners and then on to Broadafalls, crossing the Avon above the falls. Heng Lake gave us the first intimation of the sort of country and ground conditions that the prospectors of the China Clay Company had to contend with when they contemplated constructing their works here.

After examining, photographing and trying to identify the various ruins, so successfully demolished that this was not easy, we climbed to the top of the spoil heap, and there David and I performed an Ed Hillary/Sherpa Tensing act by shaking hands and congratulating each other on a mission successfully accomplished (Plate 20). Not quite Everest perhaps, but an achievement which I at least felt was something I could look back upon with no little satisfaction. The view to the north was a vast expanse of wet desolation, but I was interested to find that the leat which had been dug to fill the artificial reservoirs was still plainly visible (Plate 21). I now had the answer, by reference to a map in Wade's book, to the query that had puzzled me on the occasion of the Abbots' Way walk with Dennis and his son, when we wondered how water reached those filter beds. In fact it was not water but the output of the clay works, in solution, which was pumped through a rising main to these settling tanks for the mica and sand to be removed, before the clay was piped down to Cantrel, near Ivybridge, for final treatment. Surplus water from the filter beds was then returned to the Red Lake reservoirs via a leat which ran parallel to but above the railway track.

We had arrived here none too soon to take our photographs, which was one of the objects of the expedition, for looking to the west now the sky was darkening and threatening (Plate 22). We had no sooner descended from the spoil heap than fog enshrouded us. The railway track was a good guide to begin with, but we had to leave it when it began to curve round Brown Heath, and take a compass bearing to get to the Avon at the warrener's clapper bridge. We were clear of the fog down by the river and though the drizzle persisted we had an easy passage along the Jobbers' Path/Abbots' Way back to Cross Furzes.

Such a brief description of this walk does not do it justice. It was the camaraderie of three like minded souls that made it so memorable. There was little beauty in the scenery on such a day, rather did the sombre sky and subsequent fog give the right impression on our minds of what life was like at Red Lake when it was a working enterprise. It is difficult to imagine, in winter, a more isolated, dreary, rigorous location in which to perform one's daily work, and still have to endure it during one's leisure hours. It was in such conditions as we had experienced that on a November day in 1927 young Ivor Thompson, son of one of the employees, strayed in search of his football. Disoriented by the fog he could not find his way home. Search parties went out to look for him, but it was not until the next day that his body was found some miles away, Hemery says as far away as Dead Man's Bottom, Wade, more believably perhaps, beside the Erme. Such a tragedy emphasises the grimness of the place. The Dartmoor that we love so much, bestowing a benign demeanour one day, can claim a victim the next.

Brim Brook and the West Okement Valley

Another grim place in which to work must have been Brim Brook, just as isolated and exposed as Red Lake in the days when the tinners streamed the valley. No military road then within a mile of it.

An article by Mr. Brian Le Messurier lists a number of ruined huts on the northern moors, giving grid references for them. Four such are located in Brim Brook and others along the course of the West Okement River. On a perfect day in September 1986 we three set off from OP15 on Okement Hill in search of these huts.

We walked due west from OP15 over ground which was unpleasant and treacherous, pitted, broken up, wet, even boggy in places, and the occasional water-filled shell-hole, all had to be dodged in a zigzag course before we reached the little stream. No difficulty was experienced in locating the higher three huts, and an easy and pleasant passage followed down the left bank of the brook. At its confluence with the major river a curious coincidence occurred. We were hailed by a man who, with his son, was out letter-box hunting. We had met them before, near Plym Head, on the occasion of our initial walk to Red Lake. John and David had also crossed their path on a visit to Yes Tor. So this was the third occasion, in three far removed localities and within quite a short period of time that chance had brought us together. We were so surprised at the meeting and such a long conversation followed that we quite forgot to look for the fourth hut near here.

On our way again now, along the right bank of the West Okement River. I had been looking forward to seeing this section, where, below Great Kneeset, the river changes course abruptly, from almost due south to north-east. As one approaches the bend the great hills enfold it and there seems to be no way out for the waters. On a spit of flat ground we found the next hut, presumably the remains of a beehive hut, so small we wondered at its purpose. Here it is that the river makes its escape, turning in a graceful curve and flowing almost in the opposite direction. Gradually now the steep of the hills lessen and their sides recede to open out where a little feeder from Broad Amicombe Hole joins it. I was reminded of my walk with Dennis eight years before when we climbed into that valley on our way across Amicombe Hill to Lydford. Then we had the opposite view of the landscape that was now unfolding before us. Wonderful scenery, soft autumn colours, the sun in a pale blue sky highlighting the tors and hilltops, and in the distance was the gorge between Stenga Tor on one side and Foresland Ledge on the other. Good firm ground to walk on, the interest of another substantial ruin of a tinner's hut, one gable still standing, and a possible beehive hut nearby. Then the crossing of Lints Tor Brook and a visit to Sandy Ford.

The boundary stone here marks the limits of Okehampton and Bridestowe parishes. It also marked the limit of our association with the West Okement. We retraced our steps to Lints Tor Brook and ascended beside the little stream. At about half way the valley steepens and narrows, clitter clothing its sides, slightly reminiscent of, but not so beautiful as, Henchertraw in Red Brook. Amongst the rocks a solitary small tree had found sufficient shelter and nourishment to survive, and in its barren branches a raven or crow had built its untidy nest, the nest being far more conspicuous than the tree.

At the head of the valley, now over open ground and bearing away from the western prong of the brook's source, a gentle rise led us to Lints Tor. What a splendid view from here of the country that we had just traversed. Great Kneeset separating the valleys of Okement and Broad Amicombe Hole, and beyond it the unmistakeable rocky crown of Fur Tor. To the left of that noble pile lay the rounded hump of Cut Hill and to its right the more distant and hazier heights of Great Mis Tor. We spent some time at the rocks, resting, relaxing, making the most of everything the little tor could offer us (Plate 14).

Thence, skirting the miry head of the brook, to Dinger Tor, followed by a stony track to the col where a mire on one side gives birth to Black-a-ven Brook and another on the other side to Brim Brook. No distance now to the military road, whose hard surface contrasted sharply with the soft splashy beginning of the walk. What a mundane end to a journey which had taken us through such lovely country, into the very intimacies of Mother Nature's bosom.

PART TWO

Walks of Investigation

Walks of Investigation

Interspersed with this series of nostalgic walks were others of a more serious nature when, after reading some book or article,I would set out to see for myself what had been written about, in which case I would prefer to be on my own, for the reason already stated, that I could concentrate more fully on the subject in hand. In this way I had amassed a sizeable amount of material which I wished I could have included in my book "Follow the Leat". Thus the chapter in that book on the Devonport Leat would have benefited with what now follows.

The Devonport Leat

Apart of course from the disused part of that leat from Burrator to Plymouth, the only part of it that I had omitted, because it is not available to the general public, was the section through the Prison grounds at Princetown. This, I felt, for my own edification, should be remedied.

So in June 1986, with the permission of the Governor of H.M. Prison, I traced its course through this area, joining it at the now waymarked public path at SX603745. In general the banks of the leat are not as well maintained here as elsewhere, in some places the going was a little hazardous, space between barbed-wire fence and the leat being narrow and the ground broken. Access to the leat where the Prison farm road crosses it also presented a problem. Herds of cows in adjacent fields set up a bellowing, whether in protest or welcome at my presence I could not decide. Conditions improved after crossing the aqueduct over Blackabrook (Plate 25). And what a disappointment this aqueduct is, what can only be described as a half-section iron pipe, the leat seeming to shrink in size as it squeezes its way into it. It is, of course, similar to Iron Bridge over the River Meavy, after the leat's descent of Raddick Hill. But why, one wonders, was so much careful design and construction put into the elegant granite bridge taking the piped supply across the Cowsic, but not on these river crossings? A footbridge beside the aqueduct enables humans to cross.

Beyond this eyesore the leat curves to the south and is joined by the branch from the Blackabrook. Following this branch northwards to the weir, some three hundred yards away, the scenery became quite picturesque in a wooded area. I dallied at the weir, admired its robust construction, and reflected that this was the original source of the leat, built about 1794, the extension to the Cowsic and Dart coming some time later.

It was here that I first noticed a dry leat channel (Plate 26) west of and parallel with the Devonport Leat and followed it upstream from the weir to the road bridge. I had planned during this walk to look for any sign of the Blackbrook Leat shown on Map 11 of Bachelor's Hall Mine (page 58 Follow the Leat) and I thought perhaps this was it, for it should have originated somewhere near here. But this proved not to be so, for it remained parallel with and close to the Devonport Leat all the way to Butchery Stream (of which more later), at much too low a contour level to have been the Blackbrook Leat. Also, in this old dry leat, there are some solid well-constructed dressed granite structures (Plate 27), far too important looking for a mine leat.

Someone on the Prison Staff I felt sure must know something of the history of this leat. My curiosity emboldened me to write again to the Governor and I was rewarded with a detailed account from Mr. R.J.Joy, accompanied by a map and sketch which explained all.

The leat is in fact a catchwater drain, made by the convicts at some time after 1854, the purpose of which is to collect the foul water from the swampy land in this area and prevent it from entering the Devonport Leat. The drain is tunnelled under the leat in six places to allow the collected water to escape to the Blackabrook. The dressed granite structures at these places are retaining walls, on each side of the drain and the leat, to prevent the sides of the leat from collapsing. The stonework was cut and dressed at the Prison quarry.

I have referred to the drain as a 'dry leat' as that is how it appeared to me, the small amount of water in it not being visible from the leat path.

Mr. Joy knew nothing of the Bachelor's Hall Mine Leat. It would seem that all traces of it in the Prison grounds has been obliterated. We shall have proof later that it really did exist.

A small stream descends through the little valley where the drain finally terminates. Its source is close to the site of the former Princetown Railway Station. It passes beneath Princetown's main street and then the school grounds, which site in the early days of the Prison was where the slaughterhouse was. Hence the stream has retained the name Butchery Stream. When it reaches the Devonport Leat it is diverted into the drain and then through the last of those granite structures and so to the Blackabrook. Dave Brewer, in his interesting article on this stream in the Dartmoor Magazine No.6, relates that in 1822 the Devonport Water Company illegally diverted this stream into their leat.

Map 9 on page 56 of "Follow the Leat" shows the long detour made into this valley by the Prison Foul Leat and the Bachelor's Hall Mine Leat, and to a lesser extent by the Devonport Leat, which is spanned at this bend by two fancy iron rails. They once carried a footpath over the leat. A map of the Prison grounds, a copy of which I was kindly given by Mr. E. A. Fitch of Dartington Hall, dates from the days when it was a war prison. It shows this path and labels it 'Bridle Road'. It leads from the

Two Bridges road parallel with the leat as far as Butchery Stream where it crosses both leat and stream before curving towards the Prison. Then it crosses the Foul Leat to connect with a path from Prison to Barracks.

Very few buildings external to the prison are shown on the map and only two are named, Duchy Hotel and Bake House. However there is another which can only be the slaughterhouse, because of its position beside Butchery Stream and road. The Foul Leat is shown crossing the valley just below. I have walked a path beside this little stream on two occasions but have been unable to detect any sign of these leats on either bank.

Continuing along the Devonport Leat and a little beyond the iron rails a small jet of water flows into the leat from the side of its right bank. This originates from a spring in a field to the south of Butchery Stream.

Sewage from the prison is now piped across the Blackabrook on a multi-arched causeway and from thence across the Princetown/Two Bridges road to treatment works just above Trena Bridge, designated Oakery Bridge on OS maps, but this I feel is referring to the clapper bridge below the modern road bridge.

The Devonport Leat also crosses beneath this road, the next point of interest along its route being the Bachelor's Hall Mine. Whilst a fairly full description of this mine was given in "Follow the Leat" the tracing of the two leats associated with it had not then been fully investigated. Only faint sections of the Blackbrook (lower) leat can be traced around Bakery Hill to the north until approaching the wall beside the Princetown/Two Bridges road where it becomes quite definite (Plate 29). The Foul Leat, though somewhat disguised as it runs beside a wall in the first field, is quite well-preserved from then on. Both leats pass beneath bridging stones in the wall and continue, looking more like drainage ditches, to the very edge of the road. A few yards above them is a small car park and this should help to identify them.

It is to be regretted that the site of Bachelor's Hall Mine has now (1986) been fenced off and access to it can only be made by jumping leap-stones across Devonport Leat, to be attempted only by the fit and athletic, or from Torgate House by permission of Mr. George Langton. I did visit the site again with Mr. Langton, who informed me that a few years ago (c.1982) the capping stone of Engine Shaft fell in, leaving a gaping hole sixty feet deep, at which point the stone had lodged, still only partly way down the depth of the shaft. The shaft has now been filled in with unsightly rubbish which itself was slowly sinking.

This is a very salutary reminder never to descend into the hollows formed by filled-in or capped mine shafts. There are other instances of recent subsidences, notably at Barrack Shaft, Eylesbarrow, (I referred to this as Hawk Shaft in "Follow the Leat" but I am more inclined to think it is Barrack Shaft as it is close to the ruins of the building designated "Barrack House" on the mine map. In which case Hawk Shaft would be to the west of it, on the other side of the farm enclosure) and at air shafts at Hooten Wheals; in the gully south of Low's Shaft, and at Hensroost, both now fenced off. At the Hooten Wheals air shaft some of the wooden fence posts are hanging in the air showing that further subsidence has occurred since their erection.

The Foul Leat of course continues beyond Bachelor's Hall Mine for the mine map shows it crossing Strane Head, where "aqueduct" is printed, and then encircling Royal Hill. The next siting of its presence will be after passing through the grounds and plantation of Tor Royal along the bank of the leat.

It surprises me now that I had so often missed the evidence of the exact crossing place of Strane Head made by this leat. An embankment consisting of dry stone walling will be seen here extending away from the right bank of the leat to two quarried pits which no doubt supplied the material for it (Plate 30). The 1959 series of 1:25,000 OS maps show the two pits and a line representing the embankment, whilst the "Leisure" map depicts the embankment only as two parallel lines.

On the left bank of the leat, and in line with the embankment, a raised track of firm ground extends across the otherwise swampy valley. Here the OS maps indicate "Stepping Stones". It has been confirmed to me by Mr. Crozier of Tor Royal that this does mark the position of the so-called aqueduct, which I presume must have been a pipe laid on the embankment and raised track, the difference in levels at the two ends producing a siphoning effect as in the case of the Devonport Leat over the Cowsic River. The line of the Foul Leat in the direction of Tor Royal is identifiable at the top of the field beyond the little quarries where a fence abuts the tree line.

It is possible to trace quite long sections of the Foul Leat around Royal Hill. It will prove an interesting and enjoyable walk, taking about three hours to complete at a leisurely pace. It is suggested that the Ordnance Survey Outdoor Leisure Map No.28 is taken, for it shows the wire fence which surrounds Sir Thomas Tyrwhitt's "Cattle Park", which will be referred to in the following description of the walk, and also the contour lines in metres which will also be quoted.

At Bull Park, below Tor Royal and the Devonport Leat, a gate gives access to the moor. From the gate will be seen a sign-post, at the junction of two tracks, pointing to Hexworthy in one direction and to the Moor via Peat Cot in the other. A short distance beyond the sign-post and slightly to its left will be seen a conical boulder, conspicuous against the sky. I am indebted to Mr. Crozier for pointing out to me a short section of the Foul Leat just below and to the right (southwards) of this boulder. Northwards the track to Swincombe and Hexworthy, and the very disturbed ground beyond it, have obliterated the leat, but it would have passed near the corner of the wall of Bull Park enclosures and descended through the fields beyond. Mr. Crozier claims that under certain light conditions or when a light fall of snow covers the ground, the line of the leat is identifiable, but I can't say that I have ever been able to see it.

Now follow the short section of the leat southwards. It will not be long before it peters out and any attempt to find it over the next half mile will prove fruitless. Mr. Crozier was given to understand that during the war this area was ploughed up for cultivation. It is still in a very rough state with several drainage channels crossing it. These channels descend from a long straight ditch approximately on the 400 metre contour line which in my first investigation I mistook for the leat itself. The latter however is at a slightly lower level as will be found as one reaches the wire boundary fence where the ground improves and the shallow reed-defined leat will be re-discovered.

If one looks westward as one traverses that ploughed-up area the little embankment and the two quarried pits will be seen on the far side of Strane mire. The piped leat across the valley would have emptied its waters on the highest part of its circuit round Royal Hill; so the water would have flowed in both directions, north and south, from here.

The tracing of the leat will not be easy. In places it has been flattened beyond recognition, in which case if one looks ahead its line may possibly be seen. Frequently reeds will grow where the leat has been, or perhaps a line of greener grass will disclose its presence. Failing all else just keep to what one would consider a level contour and hope to pick up the leat again where it is more pronounced.

The wire fence which surrounds the "Cattle Park", which will be in sight for much of the walk, inhibits the tracing of the leat where it temporarily passed beyond it. Though there is a stile here and there, little joy will be found in trying to trace the leat on the far side of the fence, for the ground is rough and any sign of a leat is only conjectural.

Thus, when the fence is reached and the leat is seen to cross it, walk beside the fence in a south-easterly direction. Once over the brow of the hill the marshy head of the second prong of the Strane River will come into view, and in the distance, on the skyline, the cairn known as Brockenborough or Broken Barrow, will be seen, around which the leat passes. Disappointingly OS do not give it this name, but only mark it "Tumulus" or "Cairn".

Descend until a stile over the fence is reached. A short distance beyond the stile what looks like the leat is seen to approach the fence diagonally. However I do not think that this is a likely angle of approach and I have reason to believe that it crosses the fence about an equal distance on the higher side of the stile. When I first traced this leat two years before I had no difficulty in following its course from here to the head of the mire. Not so this time (1988). Thus will the years of winter rains take their toll and make the tracing of the leat more and more difficult. If one looks towards the head of the mire, due north, a cluster of rocks will be seen. There the leat can be picked up again, fairly well-defined now and continues so for some distance along the eastern slopes of Strane Head.

It is on this hillside, Eric Hemery writes (page 342 "High Dartmoor") that Sir Thomas Tyrwhitt had proposed to build "seven small-holdings of potentially arable land for the raising of cereal crops". It never progressed beyond the gathering together of heaps of stones and the making of a windstrew. No doubt the near presence of the Foul Leat was intended to help fertilise the land. These heaps of stones are just out of sight high up on the hill to the north-north-east of Strane Head.

As one progresses towards Brockenborough the leat deteriorates again and eventually one can only guess its course. To round the 1299ft (396m) high hill on which Brockenborough is situated, the leat, now a little below the 390m contour line, may once again have passed across the wire fence, to emerge again on the lower eastern side of Brockenborough. I have failed to find any sign of it here. North-east of Brockenborough the map indicates "Cairns & Cists", one on the near side of Lanson Brook head basin, and two on the far side. These will now be in view. The leat can be picked up again about half way between the centre of these three kistvaens and the wire fence (375m) (Plate 32). It must also have passed near the nearest of these kistvaens on its passage across the shallow valley. These kistvaens are very good examples of their kind and well-worth spending some time examining them. The burial chests are quite large and deep and the circle of stones around them very well-preserved. The area is one of undisturbed peace and tranquility, one would say an ideal place for a cemetery for the distinguished dead, for surely they must have been men of importance. I propped myself against one of their stones and prepared to enjoy my lunch. Moments later that peace and tranquillity was shattered as a jet plane passed flying very low and immediately overhead. The noise was deafening and the ground seemed to shudder at the blast, I certainly did. One cannot help but have mixed feelings about the wonderful technical achievement of these sophisticated weapons and horror at their purpose and disturbing presence.

There should be little difficulty in identifying the leat below the circles, it is quite well-preserved here, though it quickly disappears in the

24. Colin Kilvington (right) and Cyril Phillips who came back to rescue some idiot who got stuck in the mud. The idiot however took this splendid picture of his rescuers, though he thought his camera was pointing at a boundary stone below them!

25. In the Prison grounds Devonport Leat is aqueducted over Blackabrook, and is joined by the branch from that river (see page 43).

26. The sluice gate at Blackabrook weir. To the left is the foul water drain.

27. One of six granite structures supporting the banks of the Devonport Leat to allow the foul water to pass beneath (see page 44).

28. At Princetown, beyond the wall beside the road to Two Bridges, the Prison Foul Leat (top) and the Blackbrook Leat (Plate 29), both used at Bachelor's Hall Mine, are at their most prominent. The channels pass beneath the wall and extend to the roadside (see page 45).

29. The Blackbrook Leat.

30. The embankment and raised track which conducted the Foul Leat across the Devonport Leat and Strane Head on its way to Royal Hill (see page 46).

31. The ring of stones at Nun's Cross which I believe may mark a capped air shaft of Nun's Cross Mine (see page 51).

direction from which we have come. It also begins to deteriorate as one progresses round the dip in the hill to the east, when the little valley of Rue Lake comes into view. Opposite Moorlands Farm it is very pronounced and then quite substantial banking of it will be noticed as Cholake is neared.

It is evident that the leat has reached its lowest altitude here, approximately on the 360m contour line. So, would it have emptied what was left of its waters into Cholake? Until a few years ago Moorlands Farm was supplied by a leat taken off Cholake further down its course. There would obviously be objections to sewage entering their water supply. But was Moorlands in existence then? It is not indicated on the 1809 OS Map, whereas nearby Prince Hall, Dunnabridge, Brim Park and Swincombe are. The Foul Leat must have had a very short life for the Prison was only in existence as a war prison for seven years, from 1809 to 1816, and did not re-open as a convict prison until 1850, during which time Sir Thomas had put Tor Royal up for sale in 1828. He died in 1833. Thus the leat has had 172 years to deteriorate. It may seem surprising that so much of it is still to be seen, until one remembers that some of the old blowing-house leats, twice that age, are still in evidence.

The Swincombe track crosses Cholake a little below the point of entry of the Foul Leat. Between the road and the wire fence the leat is seen again, very pronounced. A nearby stile enables one to cross the fence. Little difficulty should be experienced in following it now all the way to the enclosures at Bull Park. At about half way, when one nears a re-entrant, the map indicates, once again, "Cairn & Cist", and beyond it a group of dots. The dots represent Blakey Tor, which cannot be seen from the leat, it lies below the crest of the hill. Crossing does not give it this name, but says (page 49 "Guide") that it once bore the name Colden Tor. Hemery says a document of 1291 gives the name "La Blaketor". OS are silent on the point. There are in fact *two* kistvaens to be found between the leat and the tor, difficult to find as there are so many rocks here to mislead one. Neither of them seem to have any cairn associated with them. The eastern one is in very good condition complete with capstone. The other, with rather a chunky capstone, has one end missing. It is rather strange that the earlier OS maps *do* indicate two cists here.

At Bull Park it is not possible to proceed beyond the enclosure wall. In any case as we have already learnt we are not likely to find any trace of it there. So one climbs the hill beside the wall to join the Swincombe track and so back to the start of the walk.

Fine views are obtained throughout the walk. At the start the rocks of South Hessary Tor peep over the hilltop; the attractive setting of Peat

Cot nestling in its little valley; the perfect semi-circle of Peat Cot Hill follows. Then the Swincombe valley and Ter Hill to the south.

Later, to the east, a whole range of tors, hills and valleys will provide some diversion by trying to identify them. At Cholake, looking in the opposite direction, some tinner's mounds will be seen on the skyline. Amongst them is a tinner's reservoir with two leats descending from it to further workings below.

* * * * * * *

On July 6 1985 the South West Water Authority held an Open Day at their Crownhill Water Treatment Works in Plymouth, to celebrate "Four Centuries of Water for Plymouth". Associated with this a guided walk in the vicinity of Burrator Reservoir was organised, led by Mr. Tom Gant of the Dartmoor National Park. In the course of his very informative and often amusing dissertation he introduced Mr. David Hawkings and informed us that his book on the subject of the Plymouth, Devonport and Stonehouse Leats was shortly to be published. I had previously corresponded with David on the subject of leats (see reference to him on page 72 of "Follow the Leat" where regrettably the printers have misspelt his name) and was delighted now to make his acquaintance. I knew he had this book in mind, he had told me of his difficulty in finding a publisher.

In due course the book, "Water from the Moor", appeared in the bookshops. Was ever such a small book given such a splended promotion? A reception was held at the Plymouth Guildhall, to which I received an invitation. Speeches were made by the Lord Mayor of Plymouth, by Mr. Len Hill, the then Chairman of South West Water, and by the publisher. Wine and refreshments were provided and a large gathering congratulated the author on his work.

It is a most informative and beautifully produced book. As a Plymouthian born and bred it has a fascinating appeal for me. For instance it throws more light on what I have already written about the Devonport Leat at Nun's Cross, where it disappears into the six hundred yards long tunnel. It appears that the leat makers of the 1790's made much use of the old workings of Nun's Cross Mine and that the original entrance was indeed a mine adit, now hidden by a section of walling, which can have no other purpose, across the head of a gully. At the other end of the gully the old course of the leat can still be traced back to the present working leat. One of the mining engineers at Morwellham Quay told me that he had taken advantage of an opportunity to enter the tunnel, when the water had been diverted for routine inspection, and he had found numerous galleries leading off it. No record apparently exists of how successful or otherwise the mine was, but certainly a lot of effort seems to have been put into its development, a number of shafts being sunk. H.G.Dines (The Metalliferous Mining region of South-West England) mentions Dawe's Shaft 100 yards SW of Siward's Cross, and a level driven from it for 300 fathoms ESE, passing beneath Nun's Cross Ford, and at 45 fathoms from the eastern end of the drive, almost beneath the ford, a crosscut 10 fathoms north cuts another, almost parallel, lode. This drivage must be at a deeper level than that used by the Devonport Leat. It must also have needed draining, which would have been by adit. If you walk down Drivage Bottom (not to be confused with the OS marking of it, which is placed in what is usually called Older Bottom) beyond the tunnel exit, you will come to the source of Drivage Bottom Stream. It is in a deepish cleft and the water just appears out of a hole at the bottom of the cleft. I suspect this to be the collapsed adit and is likely to have given the name Drivage to the area. It is interesting to see J.B. Swete's sketch, c.1800, of water of the Devonport Leat flowing out of a dark hole in a cliff (reproduced on page 61 of "Water from the Moor"); it has all the appearance of another adit entrance.

Dawe's Shaft can easily be identified from Siward's Cross, especially if you have a compass to check the direction of it. In the hollow of the mound is a shallow circular pit, showing probable subsidence of the filling of the shaft. To the east of it, close to the southwest corner of the farm enclosures, are two more mounds. In the hollow centre of each of them is a small circle of stones which may indicate capped air-shafts, (Plate 31). In between these mounds is a circular levelled platform having all the appearance of a whim-plat.

In 1866 the Devonport Water Company made a number of improvements to the leat, partly to overcome wastage and partly to find additional sources of water, such was the ever increasing demands on the water supply at Devonport. One of the improvements was the re-alignment of the leat at the eastern end of the tunnel at a slightly lower level, which resulted in the digging of a new section of tunnel and the construction of a proper portal for it. Presumably the portal at the western end was built at the same time.

In 1840 the Company had diverted the South Stream (what we now call Nun's Cross Brook) into the leat. After the re-alignment of the leat they rediverted the stream, taking considerably more of its water. This produced a complaint from the Whiteworks Mine whose leat also took water from this stream some way further down its course. This diversion is still in use and can be seen entering the leat near the tunnel entrance. Examination of the diverted stream will reveal an artificial channel across the valley connecting two branches of the head-waters. Traces of the route of the original diversion into the old adit entrance to the tunnel can also be identified.

At the dates above when these activities took place, there was no farm at Nun's Cross. Not until 1870 did John Hooper and his wife set up home here. If you have a copy of Worth's "Dartmoor" turn to page 414. Plate 83 shows how primitive was his little dwelling.

About two miles beyond Nun's Cross we find another modification to the leat. An article by Mr. Philip Newman in the Transactions of the Devonshire Association, Vol.119 of 1987, lists the many leats, tinner's reservoirs and openworks to be found in the Meavy, Hart Tor Brook and Newlycombe Lake valleys. In this area alone he records no less than 12 leats, 16 reservoirs and 22 openworks which the leats or reservoirs served, a quite astonishing number. In the course of looking for two of the reservoirs associated with the openwork immediately to the east of Crazywell Pool, which itself has two reservoirs, one NW and the other NE of it, I made an intriguing discovery. In writing the account of the passage of the Devonport Leat across this gully (Page 66 "Follow the Leat") I remarked on the embankment that had been constructed for the purpose. I had not noticed then that originally the leat had made a V-shaped penetration into the gully, following the contour. The channel is still deep and in good shape. At the time of my visit, after much rain, there was a fair depth of water in it. It could be that the building of the embankment was one of the improvements of 1866.

Golden Dagger

Following the publication of Tom Greeves "Tin Mines and Miners of Dartmoor", a book which has given me enormous pleasure with its evocative series of old photographs and a text which reveals so much of the working life of some of these mines and the men who laboured there, I felt compelled to revisit them. In particular was the Golden Dagger Mine which I felt had received only perfunctory treatment in "Follow the Leat".

It so happened that Peter Richardson had expressed a desire to me to make further examination of the site, so we planned a joint expedition there.

Some of my readers will remember the acknowledgement I had paid Peter for the help he had given me with my description of Hexworthy Mine. His knowledge of these old mines goes back to the days when they had not long ceased working, when there was so much to see that is denied us now. He had sometimes regaled me with his stories of his examination of them, and gave me the creeps when he described entering some of the adits. But then, I remembered, I had done something similar myself. Not a mine adit, but a comparable long dark tunnel. The year was 1933. I was stationed, in my work with Cable and Wireless, at the lonely little outpost of Ascension Island, a few degrees south of the equator in the South Atlantic, long before the days when it became famous as part of America's long range rocket testing, and more recently as a staging post in the Falklands War. We and our St. Helenian servants were the only occupants of the Island. The Royal Navy had not long before pulled out. In their days it was H.M.S. Ascension. One of their legacies was the Island water supply. On the south-east side of Green Mountain, in a precipitous ravine known as Breakneck Valley, water was struck at a depth of 30 feet below ground. Unfortunately it was on the opposite side of the mountain to Garrison. The solution was to bore a 300 yard long tunnel clear through the top of the mountain. It was started from both ends, at the same level but at a degree or two off a straight line, so that eventually the two drivings met at a slight dog-leg. This wonderful feat was effected in 1831. It was still in use in 1933. One of the things one was expected to do when stationed there was to walk through this tunnel, which was some six feet high and three feet wide. With a guide I did it, in pitch blackness for we had no light, just feeling our way along until we came to the dog-leg. An unkind trick played by the guide on a newcomer was to warn of 'a hole here' which should be jumped across. Anyone silly enough to believe it and did so would crack his head on the roof! I felt it was most unlikely that there would be a hole but must admit I trod the next yard or two rather gingerly. After rounding the dog-leg a tiny hole of light appeared in the distance and somehow we felt safer. I was quite relieved to emerge into sunshine again.

Another 'must' for the adventurous was to walk to Letter Box. A letter box on Ascension Island? Yes, there was a letter box here long before they were thought of on Dartmoor. The navigators of the seventeenth and eighteenth centuries would call at Ascension, then an uninhabited island, and there leave notes of the name of their ship and the date of their visit etc., placed in a thick glass bottle left conspicuously for subsequent callers. The tradition has been kept up. In place of the bottle a wooden letter box has been placed at a headland, appropriately named Bottle Point, at the south-east corner of the island. Although it is only eight miles or so from Garrison, as the crow flies, Green Mountain intervenes and complicates the journey. The surrounding terrain is volcanic rock and clinker of an extremely rough nature. If you take the mountain route it was five miles to the 2000ft high farm settlement and another six miles beyond to Letter Box. It was an all-day undertaking. Now, I understand, with the building of roads and airfields etc., it is nothing like such an adventure. To my chagrin I never got there. I was transferred to Capetown before an opportunity occurred to do so. For of course we were there to work, six hours a day, or night, and usually seven days a week.

Good gracious me, what has all this got to do with Golden Dagger Mine? I crave the reader's pardon for the ramblings of an old man, he just got carried away!

Before the planned walk with Peter Richardson I had accompanied a conducted tour of the Mine with the Plymouth Mineral and Mining Club, when we had followed the full length of the openwork down from the crest of the hill, near where the still open Machine Shaft and wheel-pit are situated. I felt I could find my way down there again and I knew Peter would be interested to see those remains. We set off from the Warren House Inn and walked through the scrub to where the branch from the Vitifer Leat had been carried across the gullies of Vitifer workings on wooden launders, and from there on a raised embankment to the wheel-pit. We had no difficulty in finding the wheel-pit and the fenced-in head of Machine Shaft, all very overgrown. On the occasion with the PMMC group,though the going was rough, I do not remember any great difficulty in descending beside the openwork, which was quite impressive. Now, however, our route was barred by impenetrable growth. In seeking an alternative route we got ourselves entangled in a nightmare of matted vegetation, dead branches, pits and hillocks, really awful conditions. I was apprehensive as not long before I had not been well and was not feeling fully recovered. Silently I cursed myself for my foolhardiness. For a time Peter and I got separated and I could not get an answer to my call. Babes in the wood was a thought that came to mind. Since battling through this terrible growth was tiring me out I just waited hopefully for Peter's return, which in due course, to my great relief, he did. His reconnaissance had born fruit. We eventually extricated ourselves to emerge on to a woodman's open track. It led us to the waymarked path through the forest and so back to the bottom of the openwork.

Plate 39 of Tom's book depicts a group of miners standing at the mouth of an adit. In their midst is a mine wagon on a narrow gauge track. Map 1 reproduced from "Follow the Leat", shows this tramway track leading away from the adit to a water-wheel. The site of this adit had been lost for years, buried it is said when some quarrying took place. Imagine our surprise therefore when we discovered that the adit was once more revealed (Plate 39). A cool draught of air was emitting from it, but no water. It certainly was not to be seen during the PMMC visit, a group of twenty or so enthusiasts all hunting for mineral specimens would not have missed it.

The tramway track passes the ruins of a building which was the Miners Dry, where they changed their clothes and dried them after working underground. We followed the track, crossed the Red Water

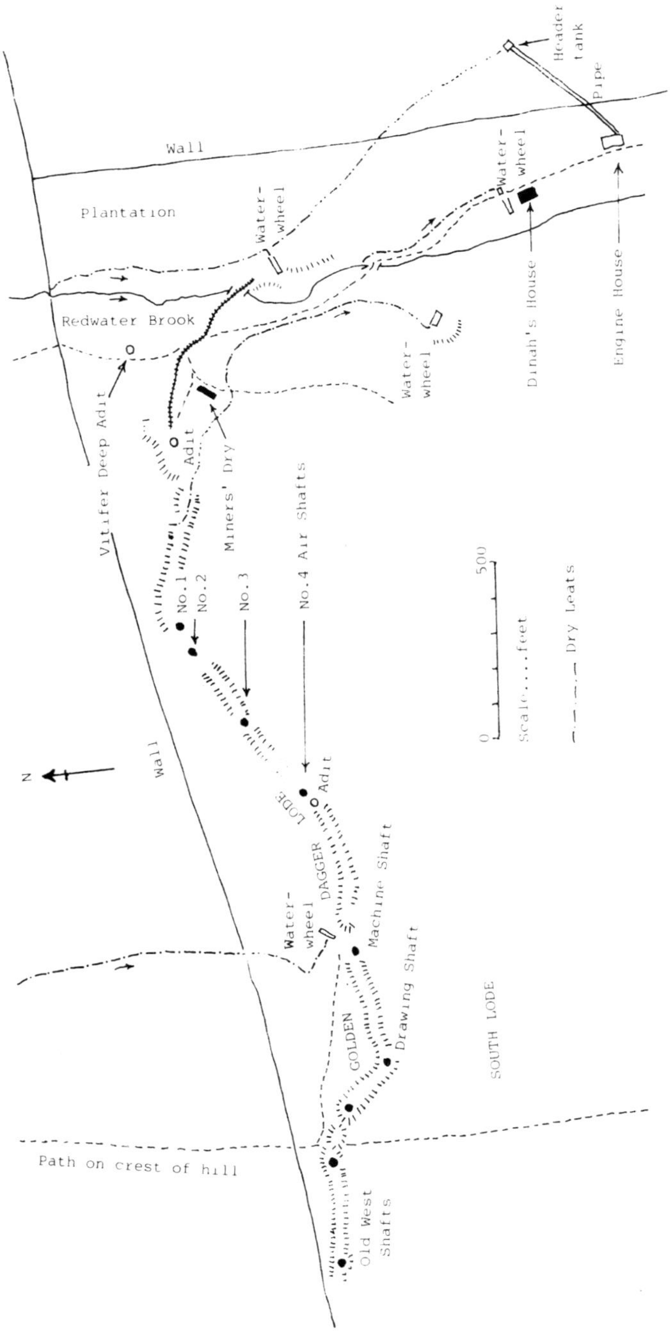

Map 1. Golden Dagger Tin Mine.

Brook on a bridge and eventually came to the wheel-pit, now barely recognisable as such. Its walled lining is nearly as broad as it is long which suggests a water-wheel of similar dimensions 22½ft x 9ft, as that which operated the sixteen head of stamps on the other side of the valley. Jutting out from the trees is a substantial embankment. I had, on a previous occasion, traced the leat to it. Its intake from the Red Water Brook occurs where that stream passes beneath the boundary wall lining the northern extremity of the plantation. Its substantial bank is plainly to be seen from the mine track running along the edge of the tree-line.

We re-crossed the stream to join the mine track which in a short distance crosses the brook on another bridge. Here a second leat commences and follows along the side of the track eventually to pass beneath it to a stone lined pit. Originally I had erroneously assumed that this housed a very small wheel. It is in fact merely the commencement of a launder to a large wheel, the outline of whose pit (30ft x 6ft approx) will be seen below, unless vegetation is hiding it, which can happen in the latter part of the summer. This lush growth of vegetation will continue to hide more and more of the remains in this valley as the years roll on. Some way further down the valley numerous buddles existed, their rotating arms driven by small water-wheels, the water for them being conducted by pipes supported on gantries. I have come across the rotting wooden stumps of these gantries but have not located any of the buddles other than the two prominent ones besides the track near the engine house. Some of them were made of wood and would probably have been dismantled.

Beyond the large wheel-pit the ruins of Dinah's House lie to the right of the track, once a comfortable residence. I was intrigued to read that a miner named Robins and his wife lived here. It is a sad tale though, for he lost his life in an accident on the mine. Over the years various other miners lived here. Plate 66 in Tom's book shows a group of people standing outside its porch. For me, that picture brings the valley to life again. They would have heard the thump-thump-thump of the stamps across the valley, and the put-put-put of the Petter engine from the Engine House a few yards down the road. In between tragedies life could have been pleasant here in spite of the heavy hard work.

On the other side of the house outside a basement which was used as a storeroom, is a little dipping well, three steps leading down to facilitate the filling of a bucket from water which still spouts from its side. A path leads from here to a clapper bridge over the stream and on to where the waterwheel and stamps shed was. Here again summer growth can hide this route.

Peter spent some time at the Engine House making notes and taking measurements for his article, whilst I took some photographs for my own records. The octagonal bases here were for the producer gas plant. The large rectangular base held the powerful gas engine. Close to it is the smaller base for the Petter engine, the pillar beside it supporting its flywheel and pulley-wheel to belt drive the dynamo. Nearby an oblong pit with a bolt at each corner is the site of an alternative source of power, a water operated turbine. The spacing of the bolts compares with those found in the small building at Vitifer (see page 82 "Follow the Leat"), and we do know now that the turbine, generator and a magnetic separator all came from Vitifer. In the interests of economy when sufficient water was available the turbine drove the generator. Emerging from a bank beside the turbine pit the end of a 15 inch diameter iron pipe will be seen. This of course conveyed the water to the turbine.

On the other side of the track, if the explorer will examine the ground carefully, some gritty black powder will be found. This is the residue of the magnetic separator, specular haematite. The iron content of the tin ore found in this area of Dartmoor had always been a source of difficulty when it came to the processing of it. In itself it apparently had little commercial value.

Peter had by now finished his investigations and I mentioned something which had puzzled me for a very long time. From where was the water obtained to drive the turbine? I really wasn't expecting him to be able to tell me, but he said "I'll show you", or words to that effect.

We walked along the path beyond the Engine House to the end of the plantation. Passing through a gate here we continued round the end of the plantation, gradually gaining height and changing course to the opposite direction, and after crossing a shallow gully, came to an oblong pit some five or six feet deep containing a large number of iron rods, the remains of a disintegrated grating that had provided a protective covering. And also, of course, at the very bottom of it the other end of that 15 inch iron pipe. This then was the header tank for the water supply, and to it a fair-sized leat channel led. We followed the course of the channel, into and through the woods, eventually arriving at the embankment above the first of the old wheel-pits that we had met. So the source of the water was the Red Water Brook, utilising and extending the leat that had previously supplied this wheel.

And so our walk, after its initial set back, ended on a triumphant note. It is always so satisfying to find an answer to questions that have eluded one for so long. We had both learnt something that day.

* * * * * * * *

Another book which appeared about this time was Eric Hemery's "Walking the Dartmoor Waterways". I have the highest regard and respect for Eric's knowledge and experience of the Moor, I had learnt a lot from him. We had corresponded on Dartmoor matters and he had visited me on several occasions, the last being at the time when he was writing this book. He had just come off the Moor, having been tracing the Grimstone and Sortridge Leat which he said was frozen solid in places. He also was looking frozen and he was glad of the warmth of my home and to partake of a cup of hot coffee. We then discussed this leat, which was the object of his visit. I gave him my views about the changes which had occurred in its course. When he left I felt that perhaps, for a change, he had learnt a little from me.

It was with a shock and genuine sadness that I read of his sudden death a few months later. Thus I feel some reluctance in criticising this book when he is not here to answer. But it was with some surprise, when the book eventually appeared, that I found his interpretation of the Grimstone Leat differed considerably from mine.

Everyone of course is entitled to have opinions on Dartmoor matters and often it will be impossible to prove one way or the other some of these controversial points. The danger in this case is that, with Eric's reputation as a Dartmoor expert and lecturer, his version may be accepted without question. I can only submit my own opinion on this leat. The reader must decide for himself which is the more convincing. I give it in the form of an article I wrote for the "Tamar" magazine, the journal of the Friends of Morwellham.

The Grimstone and Sortridge Leat

Events of the 19th Century which changed its course.

When I first took an interest in the leats of Dartmoor I was concerned principally with the better known ones, Devonport Leat, Vitifer Leat, Wheal Emma and other mining leats. In my initial book on the subject I mentioned, almost in passing, that to follow the Grimstone and Sortridge Leat (hereinafter referred to as the Grimstone Leat) would provide a pleasant walk. Little did I realise then that this leat, quite a minor one supplying two ancient Manor houses, would subsequently be of such absorbing interest for me.

Over the last century or so changes have taken place in the route that this leat has followed. In order to explain why these changes were necessary it will be best first to describe what I believe to be its original course.

Its source is the River Walkham, at a place, WNW of Great Mis Tor, where the river divides, forming an island. The presence of three blowing-houses beside the river between here and Merrivale Bridge, suggests extensive tin streaming in centuries long since passed, and this division of the river may well have been a tinner's diversion channel.

The leat, from its well-constructed weir, soon attains some height above the river and passes through the enclosures of Shillapark. Unless exceptional circumstances dictate all leats follow a gently falling contour course and thus it is possible to trace its subsequent route through the area now occupied by the quarry, on the 340m contour line. This is shown very well on the 1984 OS Leisure Map as a blue line, emerging from the western boundary wall of the quarry and then continuing parallel with the north side of the B3357 Tavistock/Merrivale road as far as Beckamoor Combe. A break occurs in the line here, for this little valley has been well streamed for tin in the past, even as late as the last century when the site was known as "Staple Tor Sett". In order to carry the leat across this valley it was necessary to build a raised causeway, much of which still remains. Beyond it the leat curves southwards, crosses the road, then skirts the eastern slopes of Barn Hill to descend a little more steeply as it approaches Windypost, as Beckamoor Cross is commonly and appropriately known, for it lies on a col between the hills and is open to all the winds that blow. From here it continued in a southerly direction, curving gently round Feather Tor and then to the east of Pu Tor, descending now more steeply again to the Sampford Spiney road where it turns westwards and runs parallel with that road to its junction with the road to Moortown. Then the leat turns southwestward over Plaster Down and so to the enclosed land of the Horrabridge area in which the two Manor Houses of Sortridge and Grimstone are situated. Sortridge Manor was built in 1558 and records of Grimstone go back even earlier, so it is safe to say that water flowed along the course of the leat just described undisturbed for several centuries until the coming of the nineteenth century.

In the Journal of the Plymouth Mineral and Mining Club, Vol.6 No.3 of 1975, there appeared an article by Tom Greeves entitled "Merrivale Bridge Mine, Wheal Fortune and Staple Tor Sett". which described a little known nineteenth century mining venture in that area. The workings of Wheal Fortune lie between the enclosures of Shillapark and Merrivale Quarry. They consist of an open-work which extends uphill from the river to the road to Shillapark. Several deep pits exist in the open-work which may indicate the presence of a shaft or two. An adit near the river still has water draining from it. Other interesting features are a substantial leat embankment leading to a filled-in wheel-pit measuring 29ft long by 5ft 6ins. wide. The outflow from this wheel is taken via a leat to another wheel-pit at the dressing-floors, a three-sided levelled enclosure containing settling-pits, characteristic of other nineteenth century tin mines on Dartmoor. The date of these workings is not known for certain but a rough idea may be assumed by an instruction dated 1859 that the lessees were not to interfere with existing leats or watercourses. This surely must have referred to the Grimstone Leat.

Above the Shillapark road a dry leat channel can be traced, in line with the leat embankment, running diagonally uphill to the Grimstone Leat, which must have been crossed by a launder, for the channel appears again beyond and continues in the same direction for a similar distance before levelling off and then following a contour line immediately above Shillapark's northwest boundary wall. It reaches the river about half a mile above the Grimstone Leat weir. This is the leat which the late Eric Hemery designated "Longford Leat" (p.1041 "High Dartmoor"), for what reason he does not make clear, though, as we shall see presently, it looks now to be a continuous leat all the way to Windypost. But it never got to Longford which is situated at the bottom of Pork Hill. A leat to Longford can be traced from Beckamoor Brook. This section just described, if it has to have a name, should surely be called Wheal Fortune Leat.

Now we come to the year, sometime between 1873 and 1880 according to Mr. Hearn of Oakley Cottage, Pu Tor, who told me that his grandfather, John Henry Hearn, helped to dig the channel to the west side of Pu Tor, the present course of the Grimstone Leat, the purpose of this diversion being to provide a source of water to the farms on this side of the Tor. No fewer than five bull's eyes are included in this section. Incidentally Mr. Hearn had never heard the word "Bull's Eye", he and his fraternity always know them as inch holes, that being the diameter of the hole drilled in a block of granite allowing a permitted amount of water to he extracted from the main leat. Of interest too is Mr. Hearn's statement that when the hole was made in the block to supply Oakley Farm a one inch jumper was used. Unfortunately this resulted in a hole one and a quarter inches in diameter, which contravening the regulations, had to be plugged and a new hole drilled using a threequarter inch jumper. The plugged hole is still to be seen. Another of these bull's eyes, at Windypost, allows a similar amount of water to be supplied to Pu Tor Cottage via the old channel.

In 1876 William Duke commenced his quarry at Merrivale. The presence of the Grimstone Leat running right across the area he proposed to quarry presented a problem. What could he do about that? Very fortunately for him the Wheal Fortune enterprise had ceased working by this time, so he had a ready-made leat above the Grimstone Leat in existence to within a few hundred yards of his proposed quarry. All he had to do was to cut a short channel from the Wheal Fortune Leat to the Grimstone Leat on the west side of his quarry. Hence the appearance now of a continuous leat from river to Windypost. This is shown on the Leisure Map as a black line, but it will be noted that it has to make a steep fall from the north side of the quarry before it can join the old course, an unusual feature in such a leat which may have caused some wonderment but for this explanation.

Mr. Warren, who has lived for most of his life at Merrivale and was working at the quarry at the time of my enquiry, told me that this bypass cut had never been used. But it seems logical to assume that it must have been, if only for a short time, whilst the initial work of the quarry was carried out, lowering the ground level here by some 60 feet. This resulted in a splendid opportunity to get some free power, by re-constituting the old Grimstone Leat and allowing it to pass over a water-wheel. The wheel operated a stone crusher; later it drove a turbine to generate electricity. The outflow of the water-wheel was now, however, at far too low a level to link up with the old course of the leat, and so a new channel had to be dug to the south of the B3357 road, the present course of the leat, crossing Beckamoor Combe on an aqueduct and receiving there a small supply from that stream before rounding Barn Hill some distance below the old cut, though meeting up with it eventually at Windypost.

There are several items of interest along this new cut south of the road. Assuming one is walking eastwards from Windypost, almost immediately a bridge of five imposts spans the leat. The interesting feature of this bridge is that two of the granite slabs bear jumper marks whereas the other three do not. I like to think that these three originally spanned the old N-S route of the leat, as part of the ancient path variously designated as Jobbers' Road, Trans Dartmoor Track (Chagford/Tavistock), Tavistock-Ashburton Packhorse Track, and Abbots' Way, all of which took the same route here past Windypost, the track being still in evidence above the leat, and particularly where the leat cuts through it between the cross and the bridge. The other two imposts of the remade bridge would probably have been added to accommodate carts.

Now, as the leat rounds the hill towards Beckamoor Combe, there is a small set stone, some 14 yards below the leat, with the letters SB engraved on the face away from the leat. A little further on a wheelwright's stone lies beside the leat, and a few yards above it the rubble of a one-time blacksmith's shop. Before William Duke started his quarry a considerable industry existed on the slopes of Pu Tor and the Staple Tors working surface granite, making setts to pave the streets of Plymouth and slabs for the pavements and market floor of Tavistock, and no doubt much more besides. The work of a blacksmith, to sharpen the tools of

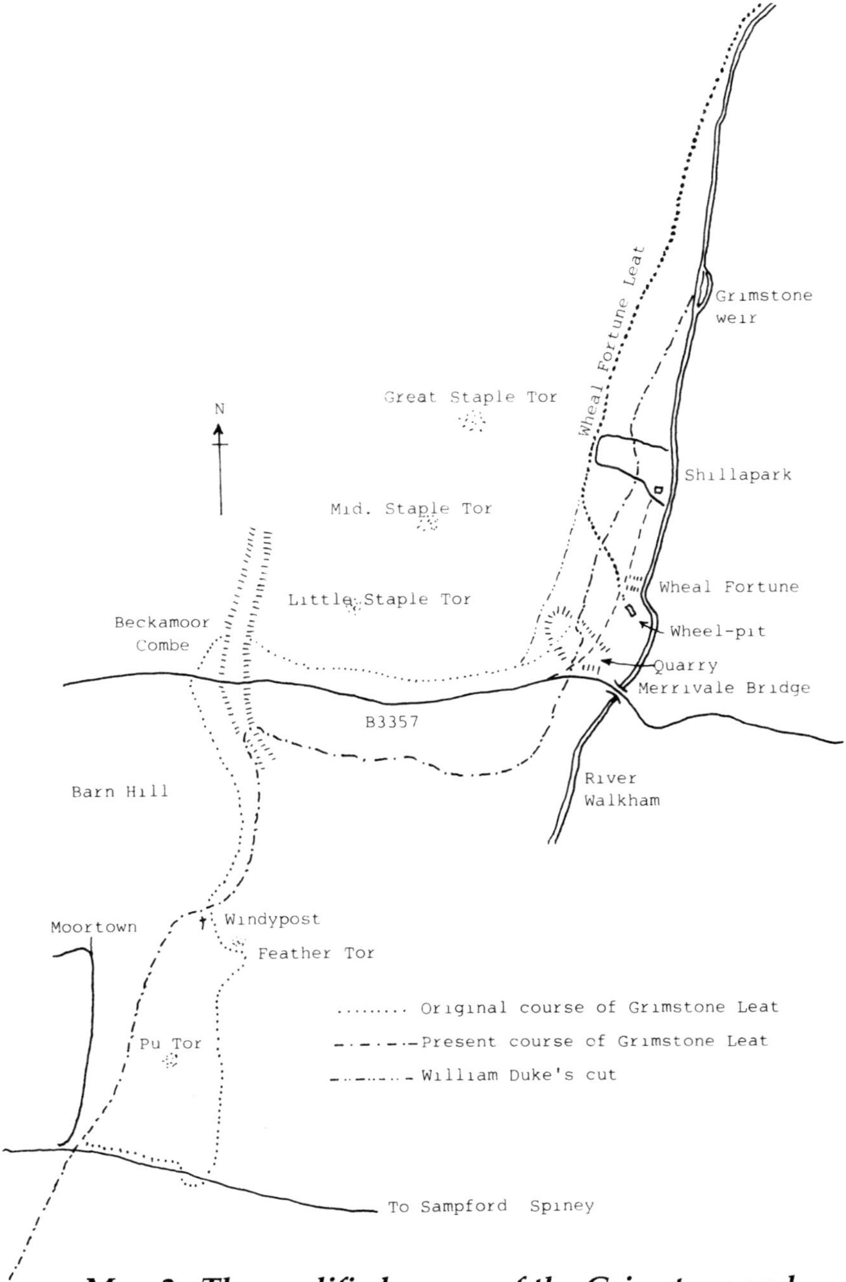

Map 2. The modified course of the Grimstone and Sortridge Leat. Not to scale.

32. The kistvaen and circle east of Lanson Brook where I was peacefully having my lunch when a jet plane shattered that illusion. The foul leat can be made out between it and the fence. Swincombe valley beyond (see page 48).

33. The splendid little arched bridge that carried PDR across Yes Tor Brook, so well built it has survived the floods and other hazards for 166 years (see page 65).

34. Yes Tor Bottom, where the tracks of the Plymouth and Dartmoor Railway and the Great Western Railway cross it, and then head for Swell Tor. At the right of the Swell Tor Quarries is seen the inclined

35. The Walkham valley at Merrivale after a light fall of snow. Top left is the commencement of a huge embankment that was intended to span the valley and to carry the Merrivale Light Railway over it. The right-

plane which the Rev. Edward Atkins Bray, vicar of Tavistock, saw working in 1831, chains and rollers being used to lower the granite to the newly constructed railway.

hand edge of the picture is approximately where the embankment would have reached the road. It does not need much imagination to visualise what a disaster that would have been had it been built (see page 67).

36. Whiteworks Mine. Possible course of the 1786 leat which had been partly destroyed by subsequent mine workings and construction of farm fields.

37. Looking in the opposite direction to Plate 36, the leat beside the farm wall whose construction may well have been made on the line of the leat, deepening it in the process (see page 74).

the stonemasons, to shoe their horses, and to rim the wheels of their carts with iron, must have been an essential part of this activity. Here, in about 1871, he built his house and plied his trade. The building stood, a ruin, until 1964 when it was demolished. (See photograph of the ruin in DPA's "A Dartmoor Century" page 53)

Beyond the combe, when the leat straightens out after its penetration into the valley, and only a few yards above the leat, are the scant remains of a longhouse. Really only its shape remains, possibly the stones of its walls were used to build up the lower bank of the leat. Not far beyond this ancient homestead there are three curious small earth-banked enclosures, two above and one below the leat. They are about the size of hut circles but definitely not such, being nearer square in shape rather than round, sunken and with short passage-ways incorporated to recesses within their banks. Eric Hemery mentions them in "High Dartmoor". page 1011, and thinks they may be associated with the longhouse. I can think of no others like them or what their purpose could have been.

Still further along the leat and close to its left bank is a huge boulder on the southern face of which is inscribed, once again, the letters SB. Are these boundary marks, and if so whose? Are there any more to be found?

Thus we puzzle over, theorise on and seek answers for the multifarious mysteries of Dartmoor. A never ending fascination.

Walking the Merrivale Light Railway

As I write this, on 5th March 1988, I reflect that it is exactly thirty-two years to the day since the last train left Yelverton Station for Princetown. Beeching's axe had fallen on one of the most historic and scenic railways in the country. Historic because the modern railway had been built largely upon the track of a horse-drawn tramway from Princetown to Plymouth's Sutton Harbour. It is a fascinating and enjoyable experience to walk the disused track and to identify the places where the old tramway, following more closely the contours, differ from the steam train's route, for the latter could not negotiate the sharp bends of the former. The moorland part of the tramway track is still remarkably well-preserved. The principal deviations are at the head of Yes Tor Brook, at King Tor, a large one at Yes Tor Bottom where it crosses the brook on a splendid little arched bridge (Plates 33, 34), and to the west of Ingra Tor. When the line approaches the Dousland/Peak Hill road the old track diverges from the other to take an entirely different route, passing through farm enclosures (an embankment is still to be seen here where the lane to Peak Hill Farm has been bridged) and crossing the road at

Yennadon Cross, i.e. the crossing of two roads, the other being the old road from Walkhampton to Sheepstor, before the days of Burrator Reservoir. It is noticeable that the road has been levelled here to facilitate the crossing of the tramway, a feature that has persisted in spite of the hundred years or more since the line closed. The track then passes through Dousland Plantation, in private grounds, but can readily be followed, after emerging from it, along the western side of Yennadon Down. When it reaches once more the track of the railway, which has traversed the eastern side of the Down, it makes a very abrupt 180° turn from east to west, and so into Dousland on much the same course as the railway. Its route through Yelverton followed closely the course of the Plymouth and Devonport Leats and on leaving Yelverton the three courses are side by side. The tramway track is easily followed across Roborough Down where several milestones will be found, one near Chub Tor being numbered 13, indicating that distance from Sutton Harbour. The first edition of OS map 1809 shows the entire route well. It must have been added in a revised issue for the tramway was not completed until 1823.

There is no better guide, I think, to the modernised route of the steam railway and its history than Anthony R. Kingdom's book "The Princetown Branch". With a wealth of detail and accompanied by some splendid photographs and maps he takes you along the ten and a half miles that the puffing engine had to pull its load around the hills and tors and open moor, in order to climb the 950 feet that separates Yelverton and Princetown. Without doubt the most spectacular part of the journey is the long loop from the Yes Tor Brook around Swell Tor and King Tor to the Foggintor Quarries. William Crossing describes this journey, in less detail but no less graphically, and he says of this section "On the slope above, to the N.E., and exactly a quarter of a mile distant, the visitor may see the railway on which he is travelling. But that portion of it is more than 200 feet above him, and it is necessary for the train to make a journey of two and a half miles to attain that elevation."

It is from the end of this long loop, below King Tor, that in 1908 a proposal was made to construct a branch line to Merrivale, with the obvious purpose of enabling the quarry owners to transport their granite. This involved the crossing of two valleys, that of the little Pila or Long Ash Brook and the more impressive valley of the Walkham. In between is the mound of Long Ash Hill with its famous collection of stone rows, kistvaens, circle and tall menhir. How were all the problems involved in building a railway across such terrain to be overcome? With this in mind, I purposed to walk this route and with the help of Mr. Kingdom's book, to find the answer.

On an early March day in 1987, when high pressure over Scandinavia kept Atlantic 'Lows' at bay, England was bathed in cloudless skies, albeit accompanied by bitingly cold winds. However, on two consecutive days these winds abated and I seized the opportunity to go out and follow the course of this little railway, just 1 mile 5 furlongs and 7½ chains in length. Useful maps accompanied the account in the book, but they had been reduced in size to such an extent that my old eyes required a magnifying class to decipher the wording. Also all distances were measured in furlongs and that required a bit of mental juggling to convert to distances that I could visualise.

My walk commenced at the little roadside sand-pit east of Merrivale Bridge, much used as a car park. Standing by the edge of the clitter just above it I faced the quarry and tried to imagine how it would be possible for the railway to cross the River Walkham (Plate 35). An elegant viaduct perhaps? But no. The book says that the road was to be crossed by a 16ft high girder bridge with a 30ft span, followed by a high embankment containing a 20ft high arch with a 25ft span over the river! A very useful contour map as well as the route maps gives the height of the rails above the bed of the river as 80ft. Thus we should have had a huge embankment here, resembling a scaled down version of the Avon Dam, with a gap in the middle only 25ft wide. Horrors! It is possible that this embankment would have obliterated the wheel-pit beside the river associated with the Merrivale Bridge Mine and some of the workings of Wheal Fortune, before the railway made a long curve around the site of Walkham Cottages (see Plate 57 DPA Centenary Book) and into the quarry, its terminus. Of interest is the name Tor Quarry given to it on the map.

The road bridge would have been sited approximately where the recently widened gateway is situated, with a Tavistock/Asburton guide stone now built into the wall on each side. One of them had formerly been used as the gate-post.

Now I faced about and followed an imaginary track southwards and envisaged myself entering a gradually deepening cutting until I reached the 1 mile point, i.e. 1 mile from the point at which it leaves the Princetown Railway at King Tor. Here the track runs close to the wall of Hillside Farm Newtake, where the little leat from the Pila Brook crosses its path. It would have been incumbent upon the Railway company to have aqueducted the leat across this cutting. About six chains beyond this point (now work that out for yourself) the cutting reaches its maximum depth of 33ft, gradually now declining until just past the tall menhir, which would have been left standing almost on the edge of the cutting. It is interesting to note that the map in the book marks two menhirs here, with a cairn between them. If there ever was a cairn here, all that now remains is the hollow of an erstwhile kistvaen and remnants of a retaining circle. The other menhir, only 10ft long, is now recumbent. One is left to wonder if it really was erect in 1908, and also whether all the stones of the kistvaen, circle, cairn and possible stone row, are now embedded in the adjacent wall.

A short distance beyond the menhir I came to the edge of a scarp which borders for some distance the tin-streamed valley here known as Long Ash Pits, through which the Pila Brook flows. In my naïveté I concluded that the presence of this quite deep scarp would have prohibited the railway from crossing the Pila Brook here, and also because it would have had to pass through enclosed land. So I followed the scarp to the point where it is shallow and a stony cutting through it leads to a ford on the brook, beyond the walls of the enclosure. This seemed to me to be the obvious crossing place and I took some photographs to illustrate it. However, as we shall see later, this proved not to be the case. The planners apparently had no qualms about driving their route through private property, or were perturbed about building long high embankments.

But by now the afternoon was drawing to a close and I had to abandon further exploration for the day.

The following afternoon I decided to trace the proposed railway in the opposite direction, from its point of junction with the Princetown Railway. This involved an initial walk from where the Pila Brook, near its source, crosses the B3357 road. Then past the ruins of the Red Houses, the still working Yellowmead Farm, the gaunt remaining walls of the quarrymen's homes at Foggintor, across Royal Oak Siding and around the head of Foggintor Mire to the Princetown Railway track; then over the col between Swell Tor and King Tor to the Swell Tor siding on the far side, a pleasant enough walk even without the added interest of industrial archaeology.

Where the Swell Tor siding arrives level with the main track is roughly the point at which the Merrivale Railway would have commenced. At first I thought the most obvious point of junction would have been where the old tramroad crosses the main track and making use of the old tramroad track, but further reference to the map shows it to be some way further back than that, where the railway is banked up to a considerable height above ground level. So it would have been necessary to bank up the Merrivale line to a similar height. This is confirmed on the contour map, which also shows that at its maximum height the embankment is breached by an arch 22ft high and 15ft span, made presumably for the same reason as the main line is similarly arched, whatever that may have been, perhaps to allow cattle and sheep to pass.

A long curve follows, the embankment declining and a cutting ensues, right through the track of the old tramway! When it emerges from this cutting it changes direction from north to northnortheast, followed by a reverse curve back to true north, on ground level now but through the dense clitter of King Tor's north slope, in which there are some very large boulders.

It is obvious now that my conjectured crossing of Pila Brook was far from correct. The railway breaches the wall of Long Ash Newtake, nearly a furlong before that wall makes a right-angled bend down to the brook. Beyond the wall another long embankment would have been necessary, reaching a height of 33ft above the little river, and passing over the far wall of the newtake about 1½ furlongs east of the menhir on Long Ash Hill, the embankment of course continuing to the top of the scarp.

There are those, and I think that I am one of them, that bewail the loss of the Princetown Line. But I am sure that we can all be thankful that the branch line to Merrivale never got beyond the planning stage. Had it been built we should now be left with two unsightly embankments. The lesser one across Pila Brook would no doubt have raised a few eyebrows but otherwise have been just an object of interest to archaeologists. But the one across the Walkham would have been an irreparable disaster of hideous proportions.

How was it then that we have been spared from this catastrophe? I am indebted to Mr. Laurie Manton of Brixham who kindly quoted for me the following notice which appeared in the Tavistock Gazette during July 1908.

"The Light Railway Commissioners will hold a public enquiry on July 20th as to the expediency of granting the application of Messrs. Duke & Co. to construct a light railway from their Merrivale quarry to Princetown. Mr. Worth with Mr Croft and Mr Prigg (the solicitor and engineer of the promoters) went over the proposed route, and found that the railway would practically isolate a portion of the Commons of Devon, and that the limit of deviation included a portion of the prehistoric antiquities at Merivale. It was therefore proposed at a Committee Meeting that Mr Burnard and Mr Worth be instructed to consult Mr W. L. Munday, the Association's solicitor, with a view to opposing the scheme at the meeting.

There the matter was hotly debated, Mr Burnard, taking up the cudgels for Dartmoor and reading a letter from the President of the Society of Antiquities deprecating the construction of the line. In spite of this the Commissioners sanctioned it, only making a proviso that it must be 200 feet away from the Menhir.

The matter of the Light Railway came before the Committee again in November 1908, when it was decided to await events before carrying the matter to the Board of Trade."

What eventually clinched the matter we do not know, but Messrs Duke & Co. must have been confident that they would get permission, for not only did they commence the embankment which was to span the Walkham valley, but they purchased the steam engine 'Ada' which had originally been used on the Devon Great Consols Mine Railway and subsequently in the construction of the Bere Alston-Callington branch line. (Booker's Industrial Archaeology of the Tamar Valley page 250).

That small section of the embankment is still to be seen (Plate 35), easily mistaken for the tipping of quarry waste. It cuts through the workings of Wheal Fortune, separating the openwork from the dressing-floors and obliterating part of the leat to the latter.

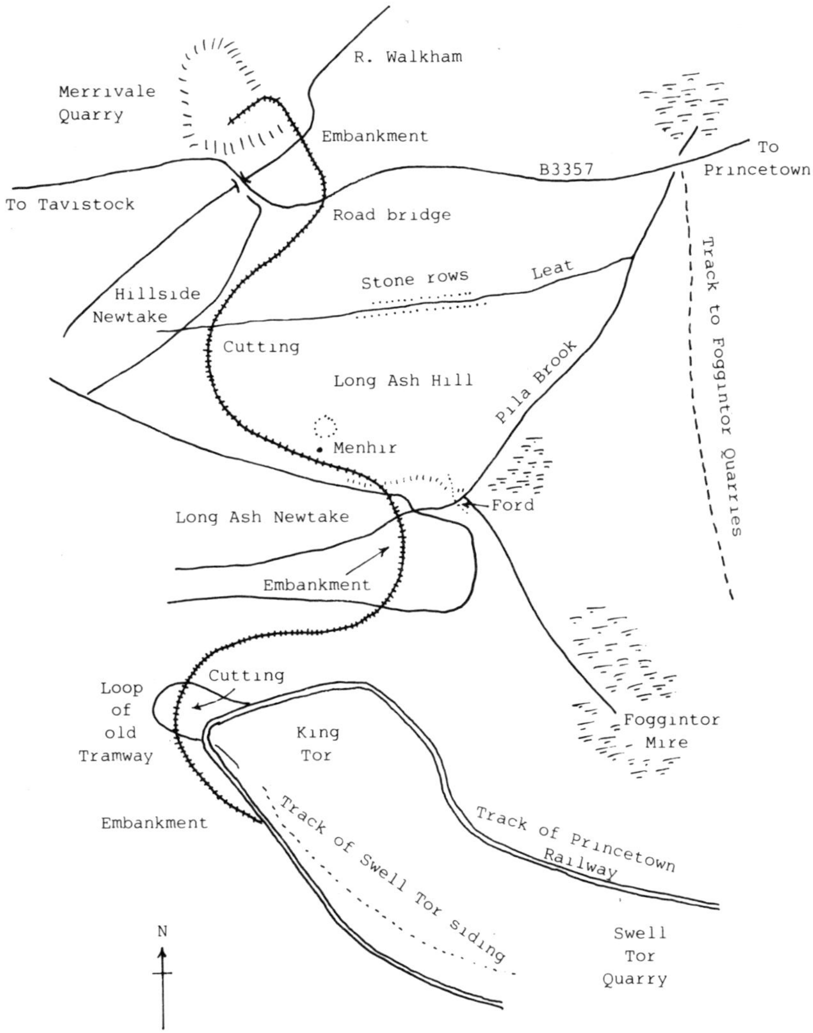

Map 3. Proposed route of Merrivale Light Railway. Not to scale.

I have frequently said that one never ceases to learn something new about Dartmoor. Some of this information comes from reading books, which is common knowledge to all; some by interchange of information such as articles and letters to the Editor in that excellent periodical "Dartmoor Magazine". Some by letters from complete strangers. Quite a lot by correspondence and discussion with friends. And a little perhaps from one's own discoveries by observation and detective work.

One cannot of course be sure that one has made an original discovery. Other people may already have formed such an opinion or made such a finding but have not made it public. And of course one's interpretation may only be based on theory and not on fact. If it is plausible it may very well be right. That is as much as one can claim. An example of this is . . .

The Whiteworks Mine Leats

I have traced the three leats that supplied Whiteworks Mine and written about them in "Follow the Leat". Two of them came from the Strane River, the lower level one ending unsatisfactorily at the boundary wall of the enclosures. The third leat came from the several streams that flow from the hills to the south, in the Fox Tor– Nun's Cross area.

We know something about these leats from historical records. In 1786 a leat was dug 1½ miles long through unenclosed land. In 1796 a second leat, 2 miles long, was dug also through unenclosed land. In 1816 a third leat was dug 1½ miles long through enclosed land.

The first and the last of these leats are much the same length, almost certainly the two from the Strane River. In the intervening years of their making Sir Thomas Tyrwhitt had constructed Tor Royal and enclosed his land; thus the third leat was passing through his enclosures. So would the first have been by 1816, but I think we shall find that once the third leat was in use the first had been abandoned. The courses of these three leats are well shown on OS "Leisure" map.

In 1985 Devon Books published, in association with Dartmoor National Park, "The Archaeology of Dartmoor from the Air", with text by Tom Greeves. Most fortunately it includes an aerial photograph of Whiteworks Mine. It shows a remarkable amount of useful detail. The relevant features as regards the leats are shown in Map 4, based on the aerial photograph, and by courtesy of West Air Photography CA.

Since leat 1, from the Strane River, could not be traced beyond the boundary wall, but the others are clearly to be seen throughout their length, it is likely that this was the original 1786 leat. Confirmation comes from the discovery of a short length of leat (4) which itself has been partially destroyed by the sinking of a subsequent shaft. The possible continuation of this section northwards is indicated on the map and on Plate 36 by a dotted line, where some evidence of a channel has been found in a more recent search. Thus it is going in the right direction to link up with leat 1.

In the opposite direction the leat leads to a cornditch wall which, as will be proved later, was built after the closure of the mine. On the other side of this wall the leat is taken along an embankment (14) to the water-wheel whose site is still to be seen but is off the area covered by the aerial photograph. A dressing-floor and buddles are also to be seen there. This I believe was the extent of the 1786 working.

Map 9 on page 56 of "Follow the Leat" shows the Leats and Lodes of Bachelor's Hall Mine, but the area covered also includes Whiteworks, where it states "£50,000 worth of Tin has been raised here". This is a large amount for those days and reflects the success of the mine in 1796, resulting presumably in the necessity for another water-wheel and stamps, and another leat (2) to operate it. This leat brought water from four little streams, Nun's Cross Brook, Whealam Stream, a streamlet from T Gert, too small to have a name, and Fox Tor Stream. In summer it is likely that the quantity of water available was not very great, so by 1816 it was decided to seek a further supply. There is evidence that an attempt was made to extend leat 2 beyond Fox Tor Stream into the Swincome River valley, but it never reached the river. It would seem that this first proposal for extra water was abandoned in favour of another leat from the Strane River, leat 3. The two combine at (5) and the water was then conducted via a long launder supported on trestle legs to a breast-shot water-wheel. The tail-race (6) from this wheel joins the end of leat section (4) and so to the lower original wheel.

Provision was always made, usually by means of a sluice gate, to divert the water from a wheel when it was desired to stop it. Thus we get a diversion leat from (5) running beside the wall (7) towards whim-plat (8). Before the whim-plat was made the diversion leat flowed in a straight line to a point beyond the junction of leat (4) and tail-race (6) to enable the lower wheel still to operate. However subsequently a new shaft (9) was sunk and the whim-plat constructed for the whim (revolving drum with verticle axle) to draw the ore. It became necessary then to cut a new semi-circular channel for the diversion leat around it, passing between it and the shaft head. This conclusion was arrived at by the examination of the aerial photograph, and later by visual inspection.

It was noticed when originally exploring the whim-plat that the pivot-stone was missing, though a slight hollow in the centre showed where

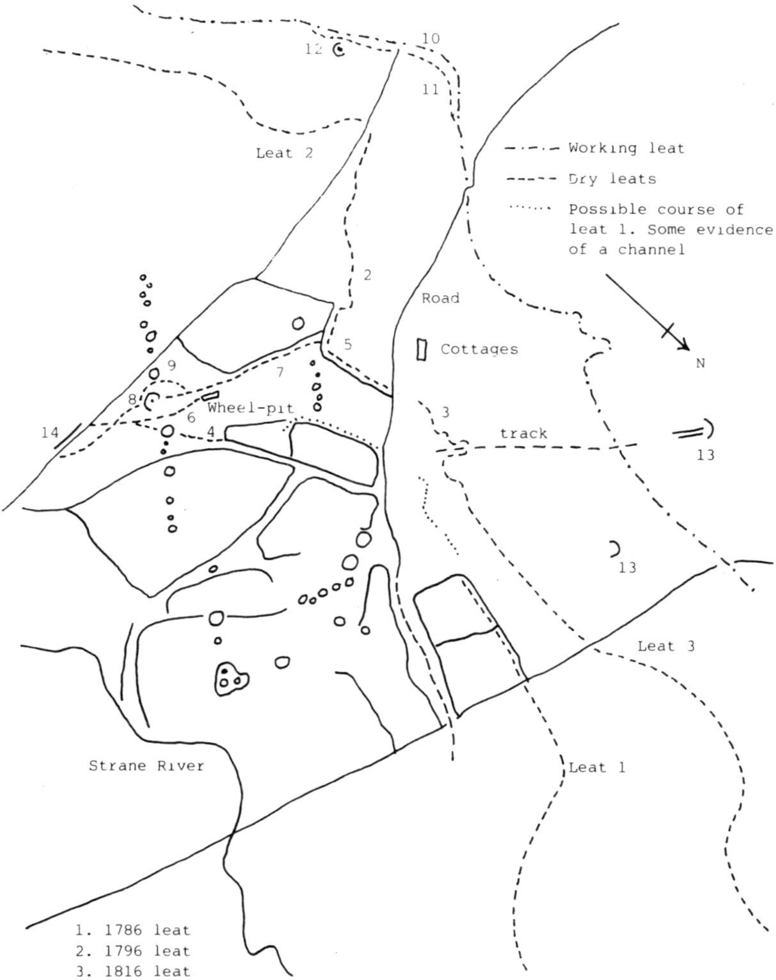

1. 1786 leat
2. 1796 leat
3. 1816 leat
4. Short remaining section of 1786 leat
5. Junction of 1796 and 1816 leats, from where a launder conveyed the water to the wheel. Also commencement of a tramway to both wheels.
6. Tail-race from upper wheel-pit
7. Diversion leat beside wall
8. Whim-plat
9. Shaft head. Roughly the position in the wall of the whim stone
10. Devonport Leat
11. Old or false cutting across head of Sunny Corner.
12. Position of cairn circle and cist. (Grandpa's Grave, p.61 Follow the Leat)
13. Adits
14. Embankment leading to lower wheel, off the picture.

Map 4. Whiteworks Mine drawn from an aerial photograph by kind permission of West Air Photography CA of Weston-Super-Mare.

it had been. In August 1987 I discovered the missing stone built into the cornditch wall nearby, where the line of pits and shafts are so graphically illustrated on the aerial photograph. The stone is only visible on the steep far side of the wall. Fortunately the side of the stone with the hole in it, some 6 inches deep and 3 inches diameter, is on the face of the wall, otherwise it would never have been possible to identify it (Plate 38).

As is so often the case, its discovery was fortuitous, for on this occasion I was looking for five other holed stones in this wall that Dave Brewer had told me about. The first of these, nearest to the gateway at the eastern end of the wall, is visible from both sides of the wall, the hole, about four inches in diameter, being drilled right through the stone. All five stones are irregular in shape, approximately four feet by three feet, and have similar sized holes. Except for the first, one can only assume that the holes penetrate the stone for the banked up side of the wall has partially filled them with earth. The stones are spaced some eight or nine yards apart.

It is tempting to associate these holed stones with the leat system at the mine, as regulators to channel the water to the desired water-wheel. But the holes seem too small for such a purpose in leats of this size. Possibly they were placed in the side of a leat to conduct water to the buddles. Has anyone any other suggestions? There can be little doubt that they were associated with the mine and were conveniently close at hand for their inclusion in the wall when it was built after the mine closed.

Holne Town Gutter

In the same category of speculative but probable discoveries come Dave Brewer's revelations concerning the Holne Town Gutter. ("Gutter" is sometimes used in place of "leat" on Dartmoor, and particularly with the Holne Leat). My first walk with David Edgley and John Pegg, already narrated on page 35, was the tracing of the Ringleshutts Mine Leat to its source at Hooten Wheals Stream. When Dave Brewer told me that his investigations had shown that this leat was originally part of the Holne Town Gutter I must confess that I was sceptical, for it is a much more important looking leat than the present working leat to Holne. But there is little doubt that he is right. The mine company it would seem took over the existing leat, widened and deepened it for their own purposes, allowing a portion of the water to flow on to Holne. Again one has no positive proof but all the evidence goes to show that it is a logical assumption. One wonders though what happened to Holne's water whilst it was being enlarged.

Dave Brewer's investigations had also revealed the site of the wheel-pit of the Ringleshutts Mine, which had always eluded me. When the leat from Hooten Wheals Stream approaches the western escarpment of Ringleshutts valley, below the point where the mine track crosses it, it will be found that the left bank of the leat has been breached, allowing the water, in its working days, to flow via a short gully to the valley floor. Further down the valley the remains of the wheel-pit will be found and traces of a building nearby. Approaching the wheel-pit is a stone-lined channel, presumably the end of the leat. This, together with the absence of any leat embankment, suggests that the wheel was of the under-shot variety. A well-preserved tail-race is bridged where a track crosses the valley.

It is assumed that a bull's eye or something similar would have been provided where the leat wall has been breached to permit some of the water to continue along the Holne Town Gutter, which is still to be seen for a short distance beyond that point as it descends to the valley floor. Vegetation, particularly bracken in summer, makes it difficult to trace the leat across the valley, but when conditions are good a likely route can be imagined. The channel anyway can be picked up again on the far valley side where it now runs a few yards above the present working channel. The two run parallel with each other for the best part of a mile but eventually converge and meet a short distance beyond the bull's eye that supplies West Stoke Farm. It is interesting to note that the West Stoke Leat extends up to the old channel, and that built into the bank of the working leat is the old granite bull's eye of the former channel.

I feel sure now that my contention, expressed on page 40 of "Follow the Leat", that the present source of the Holne Town Gutter is a mine adit, is correct. Before the mine was worked below ground there could have been very little water in Ringleshutts valley, otherwise Holne would not have gone all the way to Hooten Wheals for it. Once the mine's life ended an ample supply of water flowed from its adit which has been sufficient for Holne's needs ever since. It is possible that the present lower channel was cut then, though it is not very clear why.

Eric Hemery writes (Page 570 "High Dartmoor") "The mine relics include the large wheel-pit, to which water was leated from the upper reaches of Mardle.....". The wheel-pit discussed here cannot be called large by any stretch of the imagination. I wonder if Eric thought, as I did originally, that it was located in a gully across which are two embankments, one carrying the road up to the shaft and the other what I took to be a leat, albeit a very shallow one. At the bottom of the gully between the two embankments there is a scattering of stones which I thought may have been associated with the wheel-pit construction. There are

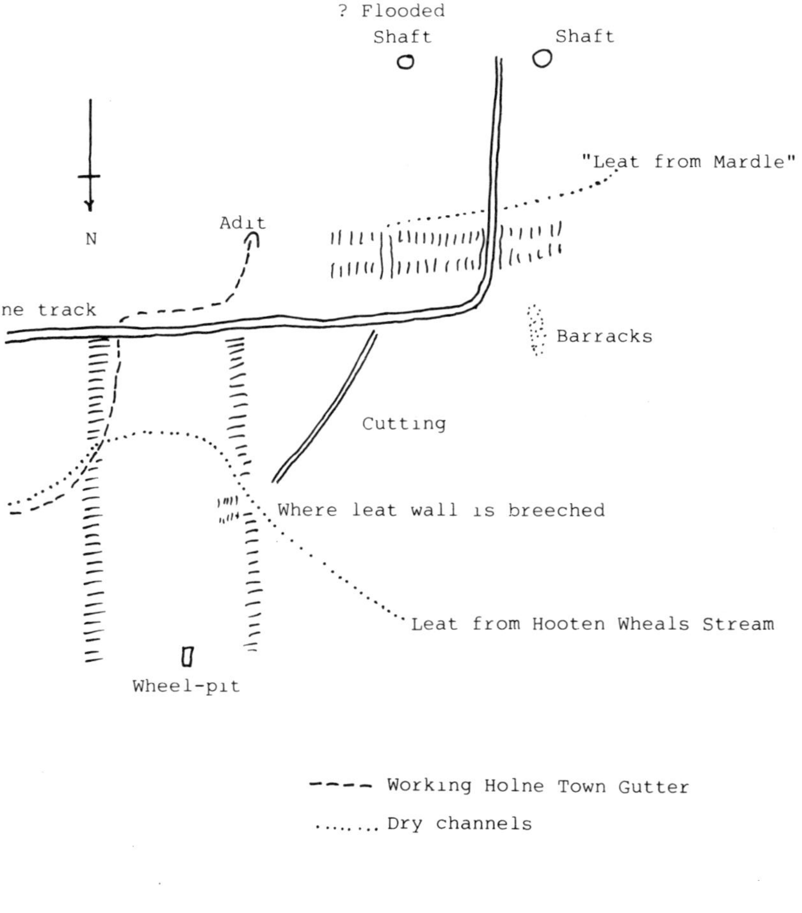

Map 5. Ringleshutts Mine. Not to scale.

38. Whiteworks Mine. The whim-stone built into the wall after the mine was closed (see page 77).

39. Peter Richardson at Golden Dagger adit, now revealed after having been buried for many years.

40. Dave and Kathy Brewer at Outer Pupers. Letter B on the rock marks the boundary of the parish of Buckfastleigh. T Gert and Wellabrook Gert are to be seen beyond it.

41. A view of the O Brook valley at Horse Ford, with the three leats, Wheal Cumston, Wheal Emma and Hamlyn's, coming from the river.

42. The picturesque water-slide on O Brook, where Wheal Cumston once took the water for its leat.

43. The built-up side of Wheal Cumston Leat, looking towards its source on the river.

44. In the opposite direction, heading towards the tunnel (see page 85).

45. Wheal Jewel Leat approaches Smallacombe Stream. Beyond the stream it can be seen heading towards tinners' streamworks and to Arms Tor (see page 94).

other examples of such wheel-pit sites. Certainly at the southern end of the latter embankment there is a definite leat which I have traced westwards, across the mine track and then via a tortuous ascent of the hill along the sides of other gullies and gerts to reach nearly to the crest of the hill, beyond which there is no further trace of it. To reach the Mardle at this altitude would have entailed going to the very head of that river where usually only dry storm-water channels are to be seen. If one assumes that this leat did extend to Dave Brewer's wheel-pit it would, after crossing the gully on that embankment, have flowed down a cutting which is in line with the embankment and ends exactly where the leat from Hooten Wheals Stream is breached and thus just at the right place to augment that supply. This theory I favoured for awhile, but on further consideration and examination of the site, I am convinced that the "leat from Mardle" never did get any water from that river, but is in fact a tinner's leat, supplied with water from a number of tinner's reservoirs (I know of one such above the site of the shaft); that it never crossed that embankment but flowed, intermittently of course when sufficient water had collected in the reservoirs (and that would have been no good for a water-wheel) into nearby gullies, typical of the surface working period and long before the nineteenth century working which we are investigating. And that the cutting referred to above, as Dave Brewer has suggested, is a tramway, the embankment across the gully being an extension of it. What a feast of leats and reservoirs await to be found in this very large area of surface workings, but for someone with younger legs than mine.

The water-wheel no doubt operated a head of stamps, and perhaps a flat-rod system to the pit-head for pumping. The route which the flat-rods took is likely to have been directly up the valley and beneath the mine track via one or other of the two bridges here. Not far from and to the east of that part of the track leading up to the shaft there is an interesting lintelled tunnel through a bank. I can think of no other reason for such a well-made tunnel other than to accommodate the flat-rods.

There was once a chimney adjacent to the mine shaft, whose base is still to be seen together with the rubble formed by its demolition. I am tempted to think that it was associated with a miners' dry, as was the chimney at Vitifer. Judging by the copious flow of water from the adit and the presence nearby of what appears to be a flooded shaft, the workings below must have been very wet. Just imagine what it must have been like to come out of the stuffy humid atmosphere below to face a freezing blast of wind on a winter's day. At Golden Dagger one of the miners is reported to have stated that after coming out of the adit there, by the time they had got to the "dry" (at that time they had to go to the

Vitifer dry a mile away) their "clothes would stand up, freezed through". No wonder they later built a dry of their own near the adit mouth.

A Gobbet Leat

Mention of the widening and deepening of an existing leat reminds me of another such case, also by a mining company.

I was returning from a walk up the Swincombe valley where I had been taking some photographs of John Bishop's house, the two Tavistock/Ashburton guide stones that are used as gateposts in the area, and also, behind a shippen of Swincombe Farm, two upright stones, rectangular and about two feet high, spaced some six inches apart, with a groove in the top of each, which I think must once have supported the axle of a grindstone. I had just passed the ruins of Gobbet blowing-house and casually looked up to my right to observe the line of the leat along the hillside which the nineteenth century Gobbet Mine had dug for their large water-wheel, when I realised that there was another possible leat below it. How was it that I had not noticed it before? I can only assume that one's eye becomes trained over the years to register more readily the presence of some relic or artefact, or possibly one has been distracted by some other more pressing concern on the previous occasions. Anyway this new find had to be investigated and I climbed up to the leat and followed it in the direction in which the water would have flowed. It came to an end near to the launder embankment of the upper leat. So it must have been in use at an earlier period and worked a smaller water-wheel, probably in the same but smaller pit. I then returned along the leat to find its source. It brought me to the service road of the Swincombe water-works which had cut right through it. On the other side of the road was the leat to Gobbet blowing-house. It had always struck me how well-preserved was this leat considering it was centuries old. The reason was now obvious, the nineteenth century miners had used it and enlarged it for their own requirements.

Visitors to the blowing-house may have been puzzled by the fact that only one mould-stone is now visible, whereas Worth (page 295 "Dartmoor") mentions that there are two. The second stone lies close beside the first but has been turned upside down. It is slightly tilted so that it is possible to see the cavity by peering beneath.

Wheal Cumston Leat

Over the hill from the Swincombe valley, Down Ridge by name, lies the valley of the O Brook. From its river does Hamlyn's Leat, marked on

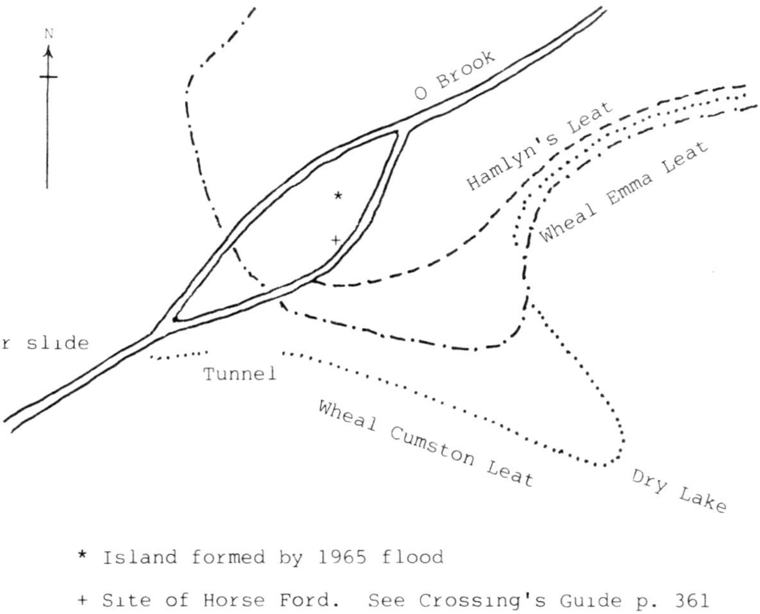

Map 6. Wheal Cumston Leat at source. Not to scale.

maps as Holne Moor Leat, take its waters. In days of yore did the Wheal Emma Leat cross it on its ten mile journey to the Mardle. The two leats run parallel with each other along the hillside. In between them is a third mystery leat, at least it was a mystery to me when I first wrote about it. I made some tentative deductions and speculated on its source which I could not find.

Eric Hemery in his "Walking the Dartmoor Waterways" has given it fuller coverage and traces it to its source on the O Brook. I should of course have realised that the O Brook must have been the only possible source of water and made a more thorough search of the area. However these were early days for me when I had only just taken an interest in leats and chose them as a subject for a book, for no one else at that time had written about them. But one does not expect parallel leats to cross one another, and that is precisely what had happened here. The Wheal Emma Leat had cut through what proved to be the older and disused leat and obliterated it at the point where it seemed to me that the leat had ended. This was something that I could not have anticipated at that time so gave it no further thought.

Some years later I read Tom Greeves' account of Wheal Cumston in TDA110 of 1978. This mine, though references to it go back to 1625, was worked underground in the early years of the nineteenth century. It is situated in the woods between Cumston (Combestone) Tor and the River Dart. I made a point of visiting it and found all the remains mentioned in the article, including a section of leat. Where, I thought, would be the source of water for this leat? Then I remembered my mystery leat and felt that it could very well be the Cumston Mine Leat. I made this suggestion to Tom Greeves and he agreed that it may well be so. Eric Hemery has come to the same conclusion.

In due course I revisited the O Brook to see for myself what I had previously missed. As I approached Dry Lake along the bank of Wheal Cumston Leat, as we will now call it, its straight line course was so blatantly obvious along the far hillside I was surprised that I had so often failed to notice it (Plate 41). Once it is realised that it crosses Wheal Emma Leat on the approach to Dry Lake there is no difficulty in tracing it as it makes a deep penetration into the valley and along the far side until one comes to the section where it is tunnelled beneath a protruding portion of the hill. The tunnel is 28 yards long, if my stretched stride is a fair measure. Along its route there are numerous pits on the surface where the tunnel has caved in. At the other end of the tunnel the leat has been walled up to support it, a feature that I had so often noticed but failed to appreciate its significance (Plates 43, 44). It makes a graceful curve towards the river where its intake point would have been on that section of the river, above the pile of rocks washed down by the 1965 flood, where the water glides over bed rock to form a delightful tree-lined water-slide (Plate 42). That flood, or others before it, has carried away any weir and flattened the reed-covered area at the river side where the leat would have been.

If this was indeed the Cumston Mine Leat, I felt there ought to be some evidence of a channel remaining where it crossed the ancient fields of Combestone Farm to the workings in the woods below them. Or perhaps one could identify the point where the Cumston Mine branch diverged from the present working channel to the farm.

I put myself in the position of the Mine Captain, who, in those early years of the nineteenth century, is preparing to go underground in the search for tin, on an ancient site where previously only surface working had taken place. Water is essential for the enterprise, but where to go for it? Nearby is Combestone Farm. In 1800 it was being worked by one Thomas May. He has a potwater leat taken off the O Brook. I cast my covetous eyes on this supply and approach the farmer with various proposals, such as deepening the leat to provide sufficient water for both mine and farm. Mr. May is not very pleased, he doesn't want a leat cutting through his fields. A compromise is reached, a solution found.

Here, I think, we have once more an existing leat being widened and deepened by the miners. (This leat must have existed long before Hamlyn cut his leat. When he did so he would have found it necessary to launder his leat over the potwater leat.)

In my investigation I walked down the leat from where it is now taken off Hamlyn's Leat to where it passes beneath the boundary wall of Combestone Farm, close to the road that leads to the farm. At this point the character of the channel changes into a typical small-capacity potwater leat; and sure enough, some seven yards before it reaches the wall, where the leat walls are flattened to give the effect of a miniature ford, I discovered, a short distance from its right bank, a broad, shallow grassy channel. It crossed beneath the road, and here I was encouraged to find that there were bridging stones on each side of the road. On the far side it headed towards the corner of the cornditch wall. The steep outer side of a cornditch wall nearly always has a ditch at the bottom of it. This, it seemed to me, provided the perfect answer for the leat, and what is more it was going in the right direction. I followed it downwards to where this wall and another cross each other at right-angles. But here the ditch ended. How disappointing. My theory seemed to have collapsed. I looked over the wall, and there, to my delight, was the channel, cutting across the angle of the two walls, the far wall having a gap in it like a sheep-creep. From my viewpoint I could not tell whether

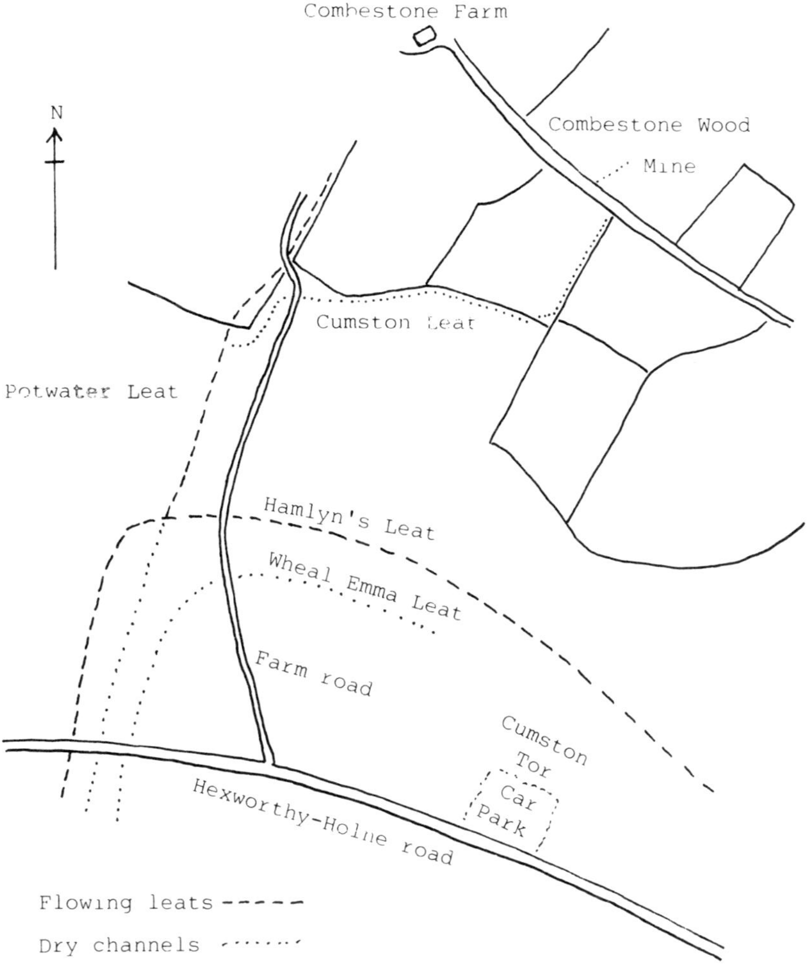

Map 7. Route of the Cumston Mine Leat through Combestone Farm fields. Not to scale.

the leat passed through the gap or what happened to it. There being no access to the fields along this wall I had perforce to descend to the farm and obtain permission from Mrs. Belsey to enter them from the bridlepath that passes between the bottom of the fields and the woods in which the mine lies. Here I found that access was possible into the field on the far side of the wall that I wished to investigate. I walked up its length as far as the sheep-creep, for that is what it proved to be, but there was no sign of the leat on this side. There was nothing for it now but to get down on my hands and knees and crawl through the sheep-creep, which fortunately was a fairly large one. I succeeded with no more harm than a mild bump on the head, and was well-repaid when I found that the leat did descend beside the wall on this side. This is not a cornditch wall of course, being an inner one, so that a ditch here could be nothing else but the leat. I continued to the bottom of the field and here the leat ended. I could see no sign of its passage through the wall, and no clues exist as to its route across the wide stroll along which the bridlepath runs, to the point on the opposite wall, some eighty yards in the direction of the farm, where the leat can be seen in the woods. We do not know of course what changes have taken place here in the 150 years or so since the mine closed and the leat was abandoned. But I felt reasonably satisfied with my investigations, which seemed to be entirely plausible, for such a route across the farmer's fields could hardly have incommoded him. Thus was the compromise effected.

It will be noticed from Map 7 that the branch to the mine comes off the potwater leat at right-angles, which confirms that the potwater leat existed before the mine was developed, otherwise, had the miners cut their own leat all the way, it would have curved gently round the contour of the hill here. It is assumed that at this extraction point there would have been a bull's eye or something similar, to allow a portion of the water to continue to the farm. Immediately above the flattened portion of the leat the banks are quite high and there is evidence of a possible barrage across the leat here, which would have raised the water-level sufficiently to carry the water across to the existing dry channel, which has the appearance of being at a slightly higher level, though levels are notoriously difficult to judge by eye. How often have we seen leats going uphill! In any case that dry channel has obviously been filled in, as has any connecting channel.

The Vitifer and Wheal Caroline Leats

Another omission of mine revealed by Eric Hemery's "Walking the Dartmoor Waterways" concerns the Vitifer Leat. In my account of what I had called the false cutting (from the River Dart at Sandy Hole) and which other writers have referred to as a ghost leat, I had stated that the two leats converged and met at a point a short distance beyond Winny's Down Traw. Eric's version however shows it extending beyond this point and that they do not meet until after they emerge from the Fernworthy Plantation, between the plantation and the north wall of Stannon Newtake. His Map 6 shows the two leats crossing each other within the plantation, on the steepish northern slopes of White Ridge. The crossing of parallel leats again! Now we have seen that this is possible on relatively level ground, but for them to cross on the side of a hill seemed to me to be most unlikely. It also seemed most unlikely that anyone could trace these leats through the densely planted trees of the forest. I felt compelled to investigate this, so on a May day in 1986 I set out to do so.

To distinguish the two cuttings I will refer to them as Caroline (the older cutting) and Vitifer, for this I think, as will be made plain later, will be the proper designation of them.

I confirmed the junction of the two leats at SX656818, Caroline being the higher one (OS only show the Vitifer Leat). I did not attempt to enter the plantation but followed its boundary wall to where they enter the plantation at SX648828. Here I discovered that Caroline was still the upper one, so that they could not have crossed within the plantation. The Caroline leat at this point is shallow but definite though it soon deteriorates into little more than a sheep track, but clumps of heather on what would have been its left (lower) bank helped to identify the line. Added confirmation came as it crossed an ancient reave, leaving a gap in the reave; and then, when the prehistoric pound on the left was neared there was quite a substantial cutting of the leat. Eric's map does in fact indicate this route but labels it "track". I could find no channel on the other side of Vitifer. Surely if the Caroline Leat had been where Eric shows it, there would have been no need to cut another leat above it, Vitifer would have made use of it. It is because Vitifer, which from all indications and probabilities was the larger and deeper one, is the lower one from the Dart that it was necessary to cut a new channel on the opposite sloping White Ridge in order to maintain a downward gradient for the passage across this otherwise level ground.

I find this a most uncharacteristic lapse on Eric's part. I can only think that he guessed the route of this section. On his own admission when he made that last visit to me, he was being pressed by the publishers to meet a publication date. I think he just had not time or opportunity under wintry conditions to make a proper investigation.

It is on this dreary swampy plain, the watershed of South Teign River and Lade Hill Brook*, that the courses of the two leats cross each other, though it is not possible to identify the Caroline Leat at the crossing point.

From the watershed it is possible to see these two leats on the hillside below Sittaford, Caroline being the higher and less conspicuous. But on the more distant slopes of Lade Hill only one leat is in evidence. The wide gully-like channel of the Varracombe/North Teign branch of Vitifer can also be seen descending the hill from the Grey Wethers. (This section is labelled "Whitehorse Leat" on an old 6" map of the district. Other parts of it are just marked "drain"!)

Not far from its junction with the Dart branch another gully-like channel meets it from the northwest. This proves to be the continuation of Caroline, for after walking up the gully for a short distance it bends sharply left and becomes a true leat bed. The two leats, as one heads southwest and then west, are widely separated to begin with, but gradually converge until the second of the two re-entrants is reached, where the broken ground has destroyed Caroline. Beyond the bad ground the only possible identification of Caroline is a path a few feet above Vitifer. And thus it remains along this steep hillside all the way to the wall which descends from Sittaford Tor to the Dart, and where, in my "Investigation of the False Cutting" I claim the two leats meet.

In the light of the following information on these leats, a fresh appraisal of their development must be made.

1. From M.G.Dickenson's article in "Devon and Cornwall Notes and Queries" we have the following statements:

   1793 Vitifer cut a leat 2 miles in length. Rev. John Swete saw a 36ft wheel worked by this leat in 1797.

   1823-25 Wheal Caroline cut a leat from the East Dart 6 miles in length.

   1831-32 Vitifer cut a leat from Teign and other small streams two miles in length.

   1831 Wheal Caroline not a success and had ceased working by this date.

2. Extract from an old document kindly quoted to me by Tom Greeves.

   Dates in brackets have been inserted by him.

   "...Richard Wadge...saith that he knows Viteford Tin Mine...that he knew the sd. mine forty years since (i.e. c.1796) - that at that time there was an old watercourse bringing water to the Mine from a distance of about two Miles - that he worked at the sd. Viteford Tin Mine

Hugh Breton refers to this brook as Ladle Brook. No doubt that is how he heard the moormen pronounce it.

about four or five years ago (i.e. c. 1831-2) - that then a Watercourse in length above two Miles was cut by the shareholders of the sd Mine whereby a part of the River Teign and some little streams of water were diverted into a leat leading to the Wheal Caroline Tin Mine in the parish of Lidford in the sd. County and from thence to the sd. Vitiford Tin Mine...And these deponents Richard Wadge and Walter Coombes further say that they know Wheal Caroline Tin Mine in the sd. parish of Lidford - that they knew when it was first worked about eleven or twelve years since (c.1824-5) - that they remember a leat cut for several miles bringing water to the said Mine..."

3. Extracts from some historical notes on Birch Tor and Vitifer:

   1797 36ft Water-wheel for pumping

   1820 Was on a large scale

   1834 Was large and profitable, being worked by Capt. John Paull

   1838 Had three wheels - 2 x 40ft., 1 x 32ft

   1846 Had 39 heads of stamps working

   1848 "On the brink of becoming the richest mine in Europe"

Sifting through this information I visualise the following sequence of events having occurred:

1796 Vitifer (Viteford) Tin Mine cut a watercourse two miles long, presumably from Stats Brook, above Stats Bridge. The leat can still be traced extending beyond Stats Brook to Coal Mires. It crosses Stats Brook valley below the eventual crossing of the extended Vitifer Leat.

c.1823 Wheal Caroline cut a leat 6 miles long, presumably the old cut from Sandy Hole on the East Dart River, and round the head of Caroline Bog to the site of the water-wheel at SX66688082.

1831 Wheal Caroline ceases working.

1831-2 Vitifer cut a leat from North Teign and Varracombe, and joined it to the Caroline Leat, i.e. at the South Teign watershed.

In subsequent years Vitifer Mine became more successful and by 1838 two 40ft wheels and one 32ft wheel were being worked. This would have required a lot more water than the old Caroline Leat would have supplied for its one wheel. Some water could be saved by abandoning the long route round Caroline Bog and the Caroline workings, by making a new cut across Stats Brook below the bog, to part of the original 2-mile long leat, its present course.

Possibly the enlargement of Caroline Leat from Sandy Hole may have been contemplated, but because of the silting problem at Sandy Hole and flood damage to the weir there, it was deemed preferable to choose a new intake point at Waterfalls and cut a new leat parallel with but at a slightly lower level than the old cutting.

The tracing of the Vitifer Leat was part of a Dartmoor Preservation Association walk in August of 1986. I had not re-walked the section between Stats Bridge and Stannon Newtake since my original investigation of it. Two items of interest were revealed here. After crossing Stats Brook, at the point where the Vitifer Leat makes a steep descent to the valley floor, there is evidence of a small tin-stamping mill, consisting of the outline of a wheel-pit, a substantial embankment above it with the slight depression of a leat channel leading back to the main leat. A rectangular bunch of reeds near the wheel-pit suggests a possible settling pit, and here a level space would have been sufficient for a small head of stamps.

The site of Caroline's main wheel in a gully was suitable only for pumping purposes, the shaft being at the head of the gully. Flat-rods could easily be routed to it. But there was no level space for stamps. So it is tempting to associate this mill with Wheal Caroline, water for the wheel being readily obtainable by taking a branch from the Caroline Leat, and which is now a part of the Vitifer Leat.

Beyond Stats Brook I was surprised to find that a heath fire in recent years had cleared the ground of the dense heather which previously I had remarked had made walking here so difficult (page 84 "Follow the Leat"). Now it was easy, the leat bed providing a pleasant path. It also revealed the fact that at the point where Caroline Leat diverges towards Caroline Bog there are two cuttings, spaced about 25 yards apart and taking parallel courses for 80 yards or so before the lower channel curves inwards to combine with the other one. The cleared ground makes them stand out conspicuously now. Both sections are of comparable size and preservation, so it is difficult to decide what advantage one route had over the other, or which of them was the finally chosen route. Perhaps there was an error in surveying and the lower one was at too low a level.

Later in the walk, where in May I had been able, albeit with some difficulty, to trace the course of the Caroline Leat from the Plantation to the South Teign watershed, the summer growth of lush grass now made it almost impossible to identify it. So the explorer should choose the winter or early spring if he wishes to trace it.

Wheal Jewel Leat

Do you remember our last walk together in "Follow the Leat"? Up the beautiful Tavy Cleave to Watern Oke? Then the Rattlebrook to Kerbeam? The Dartmoor Path to the saddle between Hare Tor and Sharp

Tor? The descent of Wallabrook to the weir from which the Wheal Jewel Leat commences? That there was a dry channel between Wallabrook and Doe Tor Brook, the implication being that the Doe Tor Brook must have been the original source of the leat?

Some years before that walk I had discovered another leat in the Lyd valley. I did not mention it because I did not know its name nor could I offer any suggestions as to its purpose. Its source was the River Lyd beneath Great Nodden. OS maps show only a small section of it from its source to Smallacombe Stream, perhaps because there is a short break in it beyond the stream. But it will be found to continue to extensive stream works where it makes a tortuous passage through the broken ground, clinging to begin with along the side of the escarpment. In one place here the bank has collapsed where a tree has been uprooted and left a cliff edge. A track through the stream works has crossed its path and destroyed it, but it is visible again running parallel with the other side of the track before, apparently, being tunnelled through a bank. After leaving the streamworks it heads away from the track towards Arms Tor and passes through a rock field and a wet area. Beyond Arms Tor a gully and the numerous tracks ascending the hill to High Down Ford interrupt it. Around the slopes of Brai Tor it has survived well. It ends on the high banked side of Doe Tor Brook.

There the matter rested, unsatisfactorily as far as I was concerned, until I received a letter from Mr. Graham Amhof of Bridestowe who was able to tell me more about it. His investigations had shown that the leat continues beyond Doe Tor Brook to the Wallabrook which it crosses and eventually joins up with the present flowing Wheal Jewel leat. So the River Lyd had been the original source of this leat. What then had been the reason for its change of course and source?

Later I arranged to meet Graham Amhof and together we walked this new (for me) part of the leat.

When a leat has to cross a river three options are available to the leat makers. To carry the leat across on a launder or aqueduct, to build a weir across the river and perhaps augment its supply, or to allow the source leat to empty its contents into the river and extract the water further down stream. This last was the method used at Doe Tor Brook. Any weir down stream has long since been washed away, but the extracting leat is plain to see. It then follows what looks like a reave, but I believe this impression is given because the leat passes through an extensive rock field and the leat makers have utilised the rocks to bank up the lower side of the leat (Plate 46).

As Wallabrook is neared a gully interrupts its course. Presumably the water was allowed to flow down the gully for the leat can be seen again

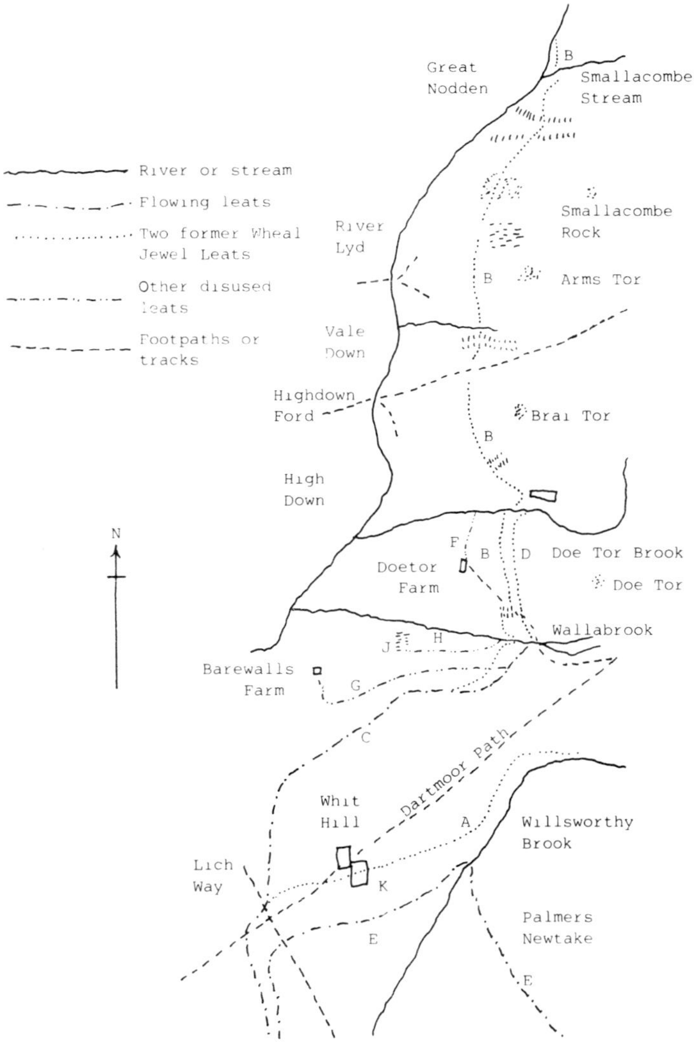

A - Leat from Willsworthy Brook

B - Leat from River Lyd

C - Flowing Wheal Jewel Leat

D - Disused upper section of flowing Wheal Jewel Leat

E - Flowing Wheal Friendship Leat

F - Doe Tor Farm potwater leat

G - Barewalls Farm potwater leat

H - Leat to Stubbly Hills gert

J - Stubley Hills gert

K - Fenced off part of firing range

Map 8. Wheal Jewel Leat.

at the end of it, continuing now beside a real wall. It soon diverges from the wall and enters the Wallabrook valley and crosses it in the form of a loop. Again no weir remains. The Ordnance Survey show this section as a black line with a staggered break at the gully on their Leisure map, but as a blue line on earlier dated maps. The higher channel here is not shown.

Beyond Wallabrook the leat enters a miry area, the source of a spring, and becomes impossible to trace, but can soon be picked up again and in about 400 yards connects up with the present working channel of the Wheal Jewel Leat. In this section it is crossed by the dry channel of Barewalls Farm potwater leat which can be traced up to but not beyond the Wheal Jewel Leat. It thus seems probable that when the potwater leat was no longer required by the Farm, its head weir and upper section became available for the Wheal Jewel miners. It must have been a relief to them to be able to abandon that long leat to the Lyd which, as we have seen, contained so many hazards and must have been a constant expense to supervise and maintain.

Wallabrook, at the height at which the weir is placed, could not have contained enough water for the mine's needs so another channel was dug to the Doe Tor Brook. Thus we get these two parallel channels connecting the two rivers. Both channels have been bridged by a cart clapper to allow communication between Doe Tor Farm and the Dartmoor Path.

Even more water was obtained for the leat from the head of Willsworthy Brook. It enters the main leat close to Willsworthy military camp.

The "Shilston Beme" Leat

It is probably well known, though it wasn't to me when I first started investigating this leat, that what we now know as the Gidleigh Leat, which has its source on the Gallaven Brook and flows through an unpleasant boggy stretch of country before passing below Scorhill stone circle and Scorhill Tor, into the enclosures of Scorhill House and out again at Berrydown stroll, where it splits into several branches, was originally part of the Bradford Pool Leat.

My first inkling of this leat was from two aerial photographs in "Archaeology of Dartmoor from the Air", published in 1985, which shows and labels the leat passing through prehistoric fields at Buttern and on Throwleigh Common. In the text which accompanies the photographs is recommended, for further reading, "The Bradford Pool Case" by L. M. Costello in Transactions of the Devonshire Association No. 113. This article I then read, but I must confess with only passing interest, for it concerned a rather complicated court case; but I did make an attempt to trace the leat on the slopes of Buttern Hill, above the fields of Creber.

By chance I met a man who presumably was connected with Creber Farm, for on my mentioning what I was looking for he explained that the leat passed through his fields. He took me into his fields and showed me a short section of it. And that was as far, at that time, as my investigations went.

Why my interest was so half-hearted then, and what sparked off a renewed interest this year, I just cannot explain. But something persuaded me to re-read that article in TDA113, this time with a great deal more concentration and resulting pleasure. What a fascinating story it makes.

Bradford Pool is now a lake of some three acres in extent, located on the opposite side of the road from Spinsters' Rock, Drewsteignton. Surrounded by trees and inaccessible, it is now all but lost to the world. But in the time of Henry VIII it was a successful tinworks, an openwork like so many on Dartmoor, but unusual in the enclosed land surrounding it. It was then known as "Shilston Beme". As is usual in this type of working a copious supply of water was essential for its operation. There being no such supply available locally it was found necessary to bring it, via a leat twelve miles in length, through areas of bog, private enclosed lands, and over valleys by means of launders, from Watern Combe on Dartmoor. Quite an astonishing undertaking and it is reputed to have cost the adventurers £1,500. What would that amount to in present-day money I wonder?

To prevent flooding of the openwork an adit drained the water to the River Teign. In the ensuing centuries this adit has become blocked, resulting in the present lake.

All went well with this mining venture until the Civil War disrupted it, as it did to all the other tin workings on Dartmoor. The leat went out of use and in the celebrated court case that followed in 1698, a farm labourer testified that he remembered ploughing it up at Gooseford, about the year 1643.

During this time, Bartholomew Gidley of Gidleigh Barton, believing that the mine would never re-open, diverted the tinners' leat, by which name it was generally known, at the "South Highway" (now known as Berrydown stroll), to irrigate his fields at Gidleigh. In 1655 he constructed a new mill in Gidleigh village to be worked by the tinners' leat. However, in 1687 the workings at Bradford were re-opened. The tinners repaired their leat and launders and re-diverted the leat at South Highway back to its original course. For the next ten years the mine prospered without interruption.

But now, in 1697, on the scene comes Bartholomew Gidley Junior, who had inherited his uncle's estate. In a high-handed manner he got his servants to divert the leat back again to his mill at Gidleigh, and to disrupt the channel to Bradford by breaking down its banks, filling the ditch with rubbish and destroying its launders.

Thus followed the court case of 1698 brought by the tinners to have their leat restored to them. The trial should have been conducted by the Stannary Parliament, in which case the tinners would no doubt have been successful, but the wily Gidley had it transferred to the Civil Courts with a jury who had no knowledge of stannary law, and with the employment of lawyers who so manipulated the proceedings that the tinners now found themselves in the unhappy position of being defendents where previously they had been plaintiffs. They lost their case. Without water the mine could not survive. That sabotaged section of leat was never to hold water again, but Gidley's section flows on to this day, some 450 years after it was first cut.

What then can we expect to find of the old leat beyond the South Highway? An intriguing map accompanies the article in TDA 113, which was presented at the trial. It shows all the relevant features from the source of the leat to its destination at Bradford Pool, but condensed and topographically distorted. However it appears to emphasise the fields through which the leat passes, "Scorul" (Scorhill House); "The South Highway where ye water is turned out of ye Tinleat to ye new Mill" (Berrydown); unnamed fields between Berrydown and Creber; and "The three fields that ye Tinleat doth run through which is on Gidley's Land", (the fields where I had been shown a section of the leat). Thus it would seem that the purpose of the map was to prove that the tinners were trespassing on Gidley's land, the crux of the matter which had reversed the roles of plaintiff and defendant. Then on the right of the map, beyond "Throwly Town" (Throwleigh), and crossing a roadway, "The Landors that carry ye water from ye Moor into ye...?... Land sum of them 22ft high and almost one quarter of a mile in length".

Also shown near here is the Zeal Mill Leat. In 1590 there had been a court case concerning the diverting of water for a Tin Mill in the Blackaton Brook away from the leat to South Zeal Mill. In 1550 there had been another similar case of diverting the water from the brook. Thus it is that the waters of Blackaton Brook were not available for the tinners at Bradford, necessitating them having to go such a great distance for their water, and probably having to launder the leat over the valley of the Blackaton Brook.

At Berrydown stroll the still-flowing leat emerges from Scorhill House enclosure wall beneath a fine bridging stone. Then from being a broad shallow stream it is condensed into a pair of pipes beneath the track. On leaving the pipe the stream divides, undoubtedly the point where the notorious diversion took place, one section still flowing to Gidleigh village, the other continuing to the bottom corner of the stroll. Originally it would have passed beneath the wall into the next field but the bridging stone has been removed and the wall badly re-made and not reaching as high as the rest of the wall. It is possible to look over it here and see immediately on the other side a short deep section of the leat. The water has now been taken through lower fields, reaching Creber at the farm gate at the bottom of Creber stroll. Its original course would have been, if the contour line on the OS Leisure Map be followed, diagonally across the upper fields to cross Creber stroll near its head. But one may look for it here in vain, the ground has been too broken up with cart tracks etc. One cannot even see it in the fields that follow, even the portion that I had been shown here would not have been recognised had it not been pointed out. But on the far side of the group of fields, at SX65738847, it should be quite readily found. It then passes between a "Chambered Cairn" and the lower wall of Square Pound and is quite close to this wall at the northern end of it. The cairn is well worth a visit, having in the centre an oblong chamber with what appears to be a doorway. I did not take measurements but 6ft x 4ft would give some idea of its size. I have not seen anything like it elsewhere.

As one nears the next enclosures above Buttern Farm the leat passes through a rock field, some massive boulders spanning the leat. On my visit tall bracken lined the leat and occasionally I had to force my way through it. Now here is a very curious thing. I have found on numerous occasions that bracken does not grow in old leat beds. The bracken may line a leat on one side only, or on both sides leaving a clear path between, as was the case here. Where I had to force my way through, it was not growing in the bed but was so tall that it was meeting and entangling overhead. We shall meet this phenomenon again, and I would also refer the reader to my book "Follow the Leat" page 148 para. 4.

Just before reaching the wall of the Buttern enclosures a mass of large boulders cover the leat, clearance I imagine from the fields, and a track beside the wall further obscures the leat. The fields that follow are those depicted in the aerial photograph quoted, Plate 6. Short sections of the leat show up faintly on the photograph. I wondered if it was possible to identify them on the ground. Certainly not by looking over the wall. Curiosity got the better of me and I must now confess to a bit of trespassing. There was no one about and no animals in the fields. A convenient gate in a lower field opened easily on releasing the catch. I *did* find traces of the leat, shallow but definite, particularly as it passes and touches the lower sides of two splendid hut circles with thick walls of large boulders.

They alone were worth the guilt of trespass.

Beyond the enclosures, at SX65558925, no difficulty was experienced in tracing the leat as far as the upper reaches of Forder Brook, where the broken wet ground, and similar conditions at the following stream, made identification impossible, where maintenance of the leat must have been a constant problem.

Above Shilstone Tor the leat can easily be found again and followed nearly to Blackaton Brook. Plate 9 of the aerial photographs shows it passing through more old fields and a settlement of hut circles. I saw nothing of them, thick bracken covered the ground and hid everything but the leat, which provided a clear pleasant path between walls of the wretched stuff, another example of bracken not growing in a leat bed.

Where and how the leat crossed the Blackaton valley, and what route it took through the ensuing enclosed country, it is impossible to say now, unless those people who live in the vicinity have any knowledge of it. In cultivated land I imagine there is little prospect of there being any remains to be seen. Some idea of its route may be gathered from the appended list of heights in metres of the leat throughout its course and at places in the in-country where it is known to have been seen.

The tracing of the leat on the high moor presented another problem. That old map gives Watern Combe as its source. This merely means that the leat at some point was taken off the Wallabrook, a river that rises at the head of Watern Combe. But where?

Eric Hemery in "High Dartmoor", page 788, mentions three leats on Headon Hill. OS do not give a name to this rounded hill that separates the valleys of Wallabrook and Gallaven Brook, and, according to Hemery, Gallaven Brook is always known as Headon River on Dartmoor. So these names I will use in describing my investigations of these three leats.

My first expedition took me to the tinner's cache on the right bank of the Headon River, opposite the present weir on the now named Gidleigh Leat. On descending the hill from Rippa Tor or Rival Tor, I noticed what looked like the line of a leat on the lower slopes of Headon, this part being known as Little Headon. I had no difficulty in finding the cache, Eric's directions making that easy. (This is the cache that my brother and I failed to find, see p.24.) A few yards above it I located the leat. Its purpose is obscure for it soon ended as it approached the re-entrant. In the opposite direction I was able to follow it to the Wallabrook, at the point where that river makes the last of its twists and turns in its descent from Wildtor Well. This I felt sure was not part of the Bradford Leat.

A photograph which I had taken on this occasion of the Headon River valley showed the line of a possible leat on the slopes of Headon on the far side of the re-entrant, and please note here, this line was the demarcation of the green area of bracken and the brown of heather and scrub above it.

My next trip to this area thus took me again to the cache and then across the re-entrant, dry and firm above the boggy lower area, to this line of demarcation. My suspicion was correct, the bracken field had not crossed this dry leat bed, which I was able to follow to the Headon River at the point about half way between Rewe Lake and the Gidleigh Weir, a most likely place to augment the flow of the Headon River. In the opposite direction it passed over the head of the re-entrant, shallow and eroded here, then to curve round the east slopes of Headon where it had a susbstantial lower bank for some distance. Disappointingly though, as I came in sight of the Wallabrook valley, it petered out. Nevertheless I felt convinced that this was indeed the Bradford Leat and that it took its waters from the Wallabrook approximately on the 400 metre contour line.

I followed the river down from a large tinner's hut beside the river, not far below Wildtor Well, as far as where another leat, the third on this hillside, is taken off the river. So I had passed the point where the Bradford weir should have been without seeing any sign of it or the leat.

This third leat is the middle one of the three on the hillside, the one mentioned by Hemery as being spanned by two clapper bridges, and taking its water to a tinner's gert in the Headon River valley. That became my return route. No question of this being the Bradford Leat, which leaves only the upper one to fulfil that role.

Since writing the above I have heard from Tom Greeves who has kindly given me precise grid references of three leats that he traced in 1975, taken off the left bank of the Wallabrook.

1. At Watern Combe at SX 6275 8720, c.1550ft (472m) above sea level.
2. At SX 6377 8742, c.1330ft (405m) above sea level.
3. At SX 6395 8735, c.1300ft (396m) above sea level.

Thus his leat 2 coincides with my estimated height of a probable position of the weir for the upper of the three leats that I had traced on Headon. His leat 1 he says could be traced round the head of Gallaven Brook to a point above Buttern Stone Circle, after which its course is not clear. Now the map presented at the court case also includes the course of a leat which supplied old Gidleigh Mill (below Gidleigh village), whose source was shown to be above that of the Bradford Leat and a route which coincides very well with Tom's description of leat 1, crossing the Bradford Leat at right-angles well to the north of the Creber enclosures.

His leat 3 is the one containing the two clapper bridges. He does not mention the lowest one around Little Headon.

All in all, this seems a satisfactory confirmation of my findings, though it must be emphasised that, after such a long period of time, this can only be conjecture, not proof.

The approximate height in metres of the Bradford Leat at various places in its course from Watern Combe to Bradford Tinworks.

Height in metres.	
500+	Watern Combe, upper reaches of the Wallabrook.
450	Wildtor Well, mentioned by Hemery as the source of the leat, but it seems to me unlikely as it necessitates a drop of nearly 50 metres to the point where a traceable leat on the east slopes of Headon reaches the Headon River between Rewe Lake and the present source of Gidleigh Leat, but which peters out before reaching the Wallabrook, its likely destination.
400	A reasonable height for a weir on Wallabrook.
380	Source on Headon River (Gallaven Brook).
372	Below Scorhill stone circle.
370	Berrydown stroll (South Highway). Creber stroll. Leat must have crossed near the head of the stroll.
365	Point of exit from North Creber fields (the "Three fields on Gidley's Land").
360	Point of exit from the fields at Buttern.
345	Above Shilstone Tor.
340	Prehistoric field system on Throwleigh Common (pinpointed by map reference on aerial photograph), followed by an unknown method of crossing the Blakkaton Brook valley near Shilley Pool, but possibly on a launder. Then a considerable drop through the ensuing enclosures. South Zeal Leat still makes a similar drop from a weir below Shilley Pool.
250	West Week, where a witness at the trial testified to seeing the wooden launders carrying the leat across the valley here. A height of 22ft (7m) above the road in this valley quite a possibility.
240	Gooseford, where a labourer ploughed up the leat in 1643. Two small feeders of Blackaton Brook would probably have been spanned by launders. OS map shows them diverted to an "Old Mill Leat", so their waters would not have been available for the mine.
225	Bradford Pool. A study of the contour lines between West Week and the Pool reveals a tortuous route for the leat.

A Memoir of George French, J.P.

In our walks of exploration and investigation, of speculation and revelation, we have found much that man of yesteryear has left behind him. We have seen what modern man has created, some to the benefit of the Moor, quite a lot to despoil it. There have been massive schemes that have changed the face of Dartmoor, such as reservoirs and artificial forests, and its peace has been shattered by guns and low flying jet planes. And we have heard or read of even more outrageous plans that mercifully we have been spared.

One who played some part and had some say in these changes if only in a very small way was George French of Postbridge. The Rev. Hugh Breton, vicar of Sheepstor in the early years of this century, knew him well and pays tribute to him in his book "The Heart of Dartmoor". I would like to conclude these walks by quoting this tribute, for it gives an insight into life on the Moor nearly a century ago, and perhaps it will put the reader into the right mood to appreciate the fantasy that follows it.

* * * * *

His Birth

This remarkable man was born and bred on Dartmoor. He was born in 1852 at Greyhound Farm, and died in the same house as that in which he was born, in February 1925. He had no schooling, as the nearest school in those days was at Widecombe, six miles away. The little education he had he gained at evening classes held at Postbridge by the late Mr. Matthew Rowse, for over fifty years Wesleyan Minister at Postbridge. George had a wonderful desire for knowledge, and never lost an opportunity of gaining information on every subject, by reading newspapers and any books he could obtain.

His Family

He was one of a large family, so he started in life without education and without any hope of advancement. He married in 1878, at the age of twenty-six, Jane Ann Arscott, of Archerton Farm, and settled down at Greyhound Farm, near the famous clapper bridge, where he spent the remainder of his life. He had three sons and two daughters.

His Work

He started work with his father at Greyhound Farm at the age of ten; afterwards he worked as a miner at Vitifer Mine for sixpence a day. For many years he had charge of some miles of the road from Two Bridges through Postbridge and eastwards. I can testify from personal knowledge of the conscientious work he did on this long stretch of road. For eighteen years I drove a good Dartmoor pony, and I was always glad when I got on to George French's section of road, as it was always so admirably kept. It is a lonely, desolate bit of road, exposed to wind and rain and mountain mist, with hardly a scrap of shelter. But the hardships of the work built up the character of this virile son of Dartmoor and prepared his great soul for the land.

Another valuable work George did was to help by his manual labour the late Rev. S. Baring-Gould and the late Robert Burnard in preserving so many of the pre-historic stone remains around Postbridge, such as those on Lakehead Hill. Probably the greatest and most outstanding work George did was the re-erecting of the Grey Wethers, involving the carting of twenty-six cartloads of stone to help trig up the stones they erected.

George French also built a number of the seemingly endless stone newtake walls, which were built to enclose the forest lands. He told me that he built the long wall that runs from Archerton along at the back of Arch Tor on to the Cherrybrook, and he was instructed not to touch the triple circle which encloses a kistvaen on the north side of the wall.

His Public Life

In public life he was very active, being Chairman of the Parish Council for twenty years, a member of the Board of Guardians, and a Justice of the Peace for Devon. It was indeed an honour to him to become a J.P. in 1912.

His Meetings with Royalty

When in 1910, the then Prince and Princess of Wales attended Huccaby Races, their Royal Highnesses expressed a desire to be introduced to a typical man of the moor. George French was introduced to them, and had a long talk with the Royal visitors.

In 1921, when the present Prince of Wales visited Dartmoor, George was invited to join the Royal party at the Royal Cornwall Show at Truro. George described it as the greatest day of his life.

Next day fell to him the honour of piloting the Prince over the moors from Postbridge to Fernworthy, where the Prince visited his tree nurseries. At the close of the day the Prince and his party honoured Mr. French and his family with their presence at tea.

His Cranmere Journeys

George for many years used to take visitors to Cranmere Pool, Fur Tor, and other remote spots in the wilds. I and a party went with him one day in June 1912. It was certainly an easy way to this remote spot. We went all of us seated in the bottom of a cart, which conveyed us over rocks, ruts, leat beds, and other obstacles to cosy transport. We passed close by Grey Wethers Circles and along the foot of the northern slopes of Sittaford Tor, then crossed the head waters of the North Teign and ascended White Horse Hill, on the top of which the horse was taken out of the cart and tethered. From here George took us straight across the bogs to the Pool, which we reached without wetting our boots that day. We returned as we came – at the bottom of George's cart, bumped, shaken and bruised, but overjoyed at having had such an unforgettable day.

One day he took a party of Londoners to Cranmere, who had no idea of the rough walk over bog and fen before them – 7 long miles of hill-climbing, and were most unsuitably dressed for such an excursion. The consequence was that one of the ladies reached the pool in a state of collapse, and was quite unable to walk any further, so George gallantly undertook to carry her on his back all the way home to Postbridge – which feat of endurance he accomplished safely.

His Knowledge of Dartmoor

He was interviewed by a representative of the Western Morning News on the subject of a proposed Hydro-Electric Supply Scheme. His knowledge of the moor, its advantages, and its people, entitled his views to be treated with respect.

Mr. French expressed opposition to the scheme under two heads – that it would be a failure, and that if carried out it would be a serious matter for the people on the moor in general. He expressed the emphatic opinion that with a storm of snow the whole thing would collapse. Snow would drift in the leats and freeze like a block of ice. That would necessarily stop the power until there was a thaw. When Devonport was dependent on the Devonport Leat for its water supply, he had known hundreds of men engaged in clearing the leat to get the water through as quickly as possible, and that was a small matter compared with the numerous leats and reservoirs which were proposed in the scheme. (Reservoirs at Fox Tor Mire and Broadmarsh were two of such proposals).

I shall never forget sitting with old George over his peat fire one winter's night, talking to him on this subject, and he was saying that it was impossible for the promoters of this electric scheme to adequately compensate him for the land they would flood. All at once his honest face became poppy red, his eyes flashed like fire, and boiling with indignation, he said: "Why sir, we should be robbed again just as we was in the old days." He evidently had some very bitter experiences of bygone years in his memory.

The tribute to George French quoted in this section is taken from the Rev. Hugh Breton's book 'The Heart of Dartmoor', published in 1926.

PART THREE

The Story of a Dartmoor Valley

Birth of a Raindrop – Death of a Dewdrop

A Story of a Dartmoor Valley

I have walked the Deancombe valley more times than I can remember. It has always fascinated me, its beauty tempered by an indefinable air of sadness. On the occasion of my first crossing the river at Dennicombe Ford, I reflected on what changes this little stream has seen, culminating in the building of Burrator Reservoir and the subsequent closing of all the farms in the area around it. Thus was the germ of an idea implanted in my mind, to remain there undeveloped but not forgotten during the ensuing years, until an enforced rest gave me the opportunity to work on it. The tale that follows is the result.

Part 1. Birth of a Raindrop. *Period circa 1830*

Storm clouds build up in the western approaches, come racing in over the coast of Cornwall, cast their shadow on the Tamar and Tavy, gather in fury over Plymouth, darken the hills of Dartmoor and there unleash their burden, saturating hill and dale, man and beast, rock and heather. The peaty soil can hold no more and water streams off the hillsides into the valleys to swell the rivers and streams into sudden spate.

The storm passes. The gloom lifts, the merciless deluge turns to gentle rain, eases to a few spattering splashes, and a final drop descends to mother earth at the very head of a broad, desolate and stone-strewn valley.

I am that raindrop. I have a tale to tell you.

Several hundred years ago this now quiet valley was the scene of great activity. Men laboured in the mire, the source of a little stream, digging into the soil, turning over the stones, discarding some, keeping other heavier ones which contained the tin-stone for which they were hunting. The result of all that labour is still plain to see, heaps of stones still as bare as when they were placed there, in spite of the intervening centuries. In some places the heaps have gathered a softening coat of soil and stunted scrub, but the undulations betray their presence. I, the raindrop, and millions of my companions thread our way through the heaps, broadening out here, gathering together there, twisting and weaving between the steep valley sides, the height of the scarp being indicative of the amount of soil which has been removed to lower the bed so that the rich tin-bearing ground could be reached[1]. For half a mile or so does this continue, until we reach the vicinity of a rock-topped hill appropriately named Combeshead Tor. Almost within its shadow prehistoric man erected a mysterious row of stones, terminating in a circle of stones within which he buried his dead. Many of the stones, including the two tallest ones near to the circle, now lie prostrate. The burial chamber has been ransacked and is now a mere hollow in a shallow mound.

By now though my scattered brethren have all come together in one cohesive stream. We become known as Combeshead Brook. The valley narrows and steepens and we tumble gaily down a miniature gorge in a series of delightful cascades, the spate due to the storm having fallen as quickly as it had risen. The centuries have not much changed our course nor the scenery around us since the days of those hunting tinners. Beyond the little gorge is further evidence of their workings, for their heaps of stones continue to litter the steep descent of this valley. Lower down still they had cut gullies into the hillside in their search for the tin-stone. In some of these gullies will be found caches, where it is possible that they hid their tools and/or the produce of their labours. It is thought that later man used some of them for the storage of vegetables and they called them potato caves. It would not be surprising if some of them hid smuggled liquor. One such cache in particular has a very small entrance and is so well concealed it is very difficult to find[2].

Near to these gullies, on the opposite bank, from another series of cascades, a channel has been dug in the ground and into it some of my companions are diverted. It is called a leat.

Shortly we come to a ford, and a little beyond it a single stone clapper bridge spans the brook. A path from the ford leads to the entrance of Combeshead Farm. Here, nearby his gate, John Pomeroy[3] is inspecting his store of root vegetables, kept cool and in good condition beneath a huge overhanging rock, the gaps around it being walled up to form a sizable chamber. Above his farmhouse, beside a track leading up the valley, is another much larger cave, made by excavating the growan beneath boulders[4]. Satisfied as to the condition of his vegetables, John now fills his bucket at a spout of water issuing from a gap in the wall between cave and gate. This is the other end of that leat and constitutes his water supply.

For some time we had been conscious of a repetitive thumping noise, getting ever louder as we progressed, a disturbing element in stark contrast to the rustic sounds of farming.

Below the clapper bridge I get caught in one of those eddies formed where rock formation holds back half of the water whilst the other half spouts through a fissure in a busy little fall. With a cheery farewell to those of my companions who continue on their way, I remain in a slowly gyrating circle of foam speckled water which gives me the opportunity to discover the source of those rhythmic beats.

A maid emerges from the porch of the farmhouse, carrying a can of steaming liquid. She trips lightly down the path to the stream, crosses it by the clapper and descends the far bank, passing me with an amused smile as she sees my captive movements. On she goes to the source of all that clatter of machinery. Then I see the wheel, turning slowly round and round, driven seemingly effortlessly by the force and weight of water filling the buckets on its rim from a wooden shute or launder attached to the high ground above. The maid leaps across the flow of water emerging from the wheel-pit and hands the can of hot tea to her brother and the bearded man he is helping. They pause in their work, sit and drink their tea and eat their croust, whilst the water-wheel continues its work. Attached to the axle of the wheel is a stout wooden shaft on which are two sets of projecting wooden pegs spaced some fifteen

46. Wheal Jewel Leat leaving Doe Tor Brook, its sides built up with the rocks of the clitter, giving it the appearance of a reave. Brai Tor beyond (see page 94).

47. Combeshead Brook cascading down the upper little gorge.

48. Hingston Hill stone row, and beyond it the source of Combeshead Brook, where Raindrop and Dewdrop were born.

49. Tinners' heaps in Combeshead valley.

50. Dennicombe Ford and clapper, and the flooded lane leading to Deancombe Farm.

51. Track from Deancombe Farm leading to the ford. The valley of Outcombe Brook in the distance.

inches apart. The pegs in their rotation lift, alternately, two heavy baulks of timber mounted in a wooden frame, which, when released, fall on to a mortar stone whereon the tin ore is placed to be crushed into a fine powder. This is the source of all that noise we heard, that regular thump thump thump.

So the search for tin still goes on in this valley. On the principle, I suppose, that where the tinners of old had dug open trenches into the hillside, there below must be more tin, so the miners of today go underground for it. Not far from the water-wheel a tunnel has been dug into the hill, a level or adit they call it, in order to reach the narrow veins of tin-stuff which only they in their wisdom and years of experience can recognise. Then, with pick and muscle power and by the light of a flickering candle, they extract the ore. Water dripping from the sides and roof of the tunnel is allowed to escape, for though called a level it is always dug at a slight gradient. Hot dirty work it is, and when their core or stint is over they change their working clothes and dry them in the little shelter they have built above the stamping floor.

Man and boy at the mill, having finished their croust, resume the work of feeding ore to the mortars and directing the crushed powder to two settling pits, where a continuous flow of water allows the heavy metal to sink and settle on the bottom of the pit whilst the gangue or waste material is channelled away. It is the boy's job, he is called the buddle boy, to stand in the pit to work the slime with his feet and stir the residue with a shovel.

The maid leaves them, and in passing me on her way back to the farm, pauses to look once again at the eddy in which I am trapped. She puts her hand in the water and gives it a little stir. Thus am I released to resume my journey, which immediately becomes a headlong dash amongst huge boulders, hidden to the world amongst trees, hissing and splashing in a last wild leap of joy before emerging into open pastoral country where we are joined by a companion stream and assume its name, Deancombe Brook, even though we are contributing the greater volume of water. This brook has also experienced its series of leaping cascades and from them has the leat been taken which conducts the water to the mill[5].

Now, with the added strength of our new companion, we assume a greater dignity and glide gracefully and contentedly along the gently falling broad valley of Deancombe. The rocky steep on our right, above Combeshead Farm, leads the eye up to a solitary conical rock conspicuous above a tumbled mass of huge boulders. Here the cuckoo is wont to perch and with its cry herald the coming of spring. The left valley side is open grassland hedged by dry stone walling. Running diagonally up this slope a path has been terraced, almost a sunken lane, giving access to the heights above and to the village and church of Sheepstor, a mile or so beyond. It also enables the miners to reach another adit and small shaft at the head of Outcombe Brook valley.

The dry stone walls were made by the founder of Outcombe Farm, but the fields and farm have long since been abandoned, the ruin of the farmhouse lying at the foot of the hillside, with its gatepost still standing nearby. Not far beyond another ruin, even older, lies nearer the river, where the tinners of old brought their ore for crushing and smelting. Mortar stones and a crazing millstone lie within the building and abandoned mortar stones without[6].

On the other side of the valley now comes into view a cluster of buildings constituting Deancombe Farm. Smoke rises from the chimney of one of the buildings where Richard Andrew's wife is making ready the midday meal for her husband who is expected back any moment from his visit to Kingsett, outover to Nillacombe, where James Deacon has recently taken over the tenancy following the decline of Eylesbarrow Mine, where he was captain[7]. She comes to the door and looks towards the lane which runs up between the fields towards Down Tor. 'Tis a fascinating old lane, steep and winding, tree-lined and stony, but the quickest way to the farms in the Nillacombe valley. She calls to Thomas Fairweather and asks him if there is any sign of Richard. He looks up from his work and shakes his head. He is busy forking down hay from the haystack perched clear of the ground on staddles, then carrying it to the shippen ready for the cows when his partner, Henry Bradridge, brings them in for milking[8]. Poor and primitive buildings they are, yet picturesque, and the scene is one of peace and contentment, for this is their valley, they know no other sort of existence, and on such a day as this, sunshine after the storm, why should it be otherwise?

We are approaching a ford from where a lane leads up to the farm; Dennicombe Ford they call it, for that is how they pronounce the word; Dennicombe. How much softer that sounds than Deancombe, something almost affectionate about it. Children are playing beside the river, or two of them are, whilst the eldest is busy washing clothes. We say hello to them, but they do not hear us, or perhaps they do not understand our liquid talk. We pass beneath a single stone clapper bridge and a little way beyond receive some new friends from Outcombe Brook. This name of course they also soften and call it Outam.

From the ford onwards we cease to be known as Deancombe Brook, we become the Narrator Brook. At the top of the steep hill on our left are two rather insignificant little tors, Rough Tor and Narrow Tor[9]. On the plain below the latter tor lies another farmstead which was named after the tor, Narrator Farm, and so the brook took that name also. Well, perhaps it was the other way round, who can tell, it was all so long ago.

These very names, so pronounced, epitomise the beauty and tranquility of this lovely valley. But, as if to belie that thought, another little low-lying tor on our right goes by the name of Snappers Tor, whose rocks stick up like the protruding teeth of a bulldog, crouching on guard over the farm below. Middleworth is the name of the farm, as attractive in its setting as the others in the valley.

A figure on horseback emerges from the cluster of little buildings. It is Henry Pearse[10]. He is setting out on an inspection of his flocks, for it is the lambing season and the welfare of ewe and offspring is his prime concern at the moment. Accompanied by his dog, the little group descends to the river and with a rattle of iron-shod hooves on pebbles the pony places his forefeet into the river, stretches down his neck and slakes his thirst, whilst the dog bounds into the water in a fruitless chase of a wagtail which had been bold enough to perch on a boulder midstream.

With a vigorous shake of his whole body the dog dries himself and contentedly follows master and horse on the rounds of the fields.

What a patchwork pattern these fields present to the eye, extending up the hillside to the very rocks of Down Tor's noble head. The tinners of old have been working even this far down the valley, for a deep gert scars the hill amongst the fields. As I am carried effortlessly along, quite unable to control my destiny, I contemplate on the labour envolved in the cutting of the gert and the building of all those walls that enclose the fields.

A lane threads its way along the valley floor, leading to Deancombe Farm in one direction and to Norsworthy and Vennilake in the other. Thus is social contact maintained between the communities of these scattered farms, and on Sundays the attendance of service at their mother church of Sheepstor.

I must not forget though that I am a mere raindrop in the swelling tide of water now entering the larger valley of the Mew, which already has received a contribution from the Nillacombe Lake[11]. What will be my fate now as we assume the grander title of a river. The towering masses of Sheeps Tor on one side and Lether Tor and Sharpitor on the other, emphasise the importance of the expanding landscape. The gently sloping hills are far removed from our banks and we feel a little lost in the grandeur of the prospect that now opens out before us. We snake our way down the centre, the promontory of the ancient manor of Longstone jutting out ahead. The leat which supplies the occupant of that house, now a farm, with water from the River Plym many miles away, deposits its unwanted volume into our river. Only a short distance further on a weir spans the river and checks our flow. Some of my companions disappear over the top of the weir, to continue on their way, past Longstone, neath Sheepstor Bridge, dropping ever more steeply into the depths of the gorge under Beara Tor[12], onwards ever onwards to join Plym and eventually to reach the sea at Plymouth.

My fate at the weir is to be diverted into what must be the most famous leat of all time, Drake's Leat. It had already been in existence for over two hundred years when I entered it, still taking water a distance of seventeen miles to the growing town of Plymouth. During that long period its original earth banks had been steadily improved and re-inforced, its bed kept clear of weeds and debris, and armies of labourers employed to clear it of ice and snow when winter's grip threatened to interrupt its supply. Here was old George Shillibeer[13], accompanied by his son William, walking along the leat side noting what needed to be done for its maintenance. Nearly forty years ago he had been appointed Superintendent of the leat between its head weir and Jump, at the out-skirts of Plymouth where moorland ends and the cultivated in-country commences; a necessary appointment for not only nature threatened the leat, it needed protection from the pilfering of its precious contents from all and sundry on its long exposed moorland course. With a few final words of instruction George left us as we passed beneath the road to Sheepstor Bridge. He waved to his son from the parapet of that pictu-resque leaf-clad bridge[14], for William was to accompany us as far as the launder at the gorge, to make sure that all was well there. This precipi-tous gorge presented the biggest problem to the original leat makers, how to get the water round its granite cliff-face. The difficulty was over-come by building a wooden launder around it, a no mean engineering feat. The relative short life-span of a wooden structure had necessitated its replacement by a more solid masonry construction[15], as we found when we passed over it, the sound of our erstwhile companions tum-bling down amongst the rocks in the depths below reaching us as we slid quietly above this frightening abyss. We breathed a sigh of relief as we regained solid ground and reached the wooded slopes of the steep-sided valley, the river already a hundred feet below.

For mile after mile now we wend our way, passing beside the little settlement of Elfordtown, beyond which we found we had a companion leat following the same course and within a few yards of us. This is Dock Leat, for Plymouth's growing neighbour, the Naval Dockyard, had need of its own supply and had found it necessary to go even further for its source of water, twenty-seven miles in all to the River Dart above Two Bridges. We were having a whispered conversation with each other, sharing the experiences of our travels, when the blissful peace was broken into by a harsh rumbling and squeaking of metal against metal, men shouting and horses snorting. When we reached the source of all this commotion we found it to be a horse-drawn wagon train, hauling its load of granite from quarries near Princetown to Plymouth's Sutton Harbour, much of it destined to be used for the building of a breakwater across the mouth of Plymouth Sound[16].

Conversation between leat and leat had to cease anyway now as the two drew away from each other, to follow different courses. Meanwhile, perforce, we had to tolerate the distracting brashness of our new companions as we travelled, side by side, towards a low-roofed building. To our relief the wagon train stopped at the building for a change of horses. This is Sir Thomas Tyrwhitt's wharf at Clearbrook. Not so many years ago this wharf was the scene of great jubilation, when a large concourse of people were treated to a celebratory meal on the occasion of the opening of this railway[17].

But in any case now we leave the railway track to make a loop detour to circumvent a slight rise of ground, whereas the railway cuts across the head of the loop. We re-join it for a short distance before passing under it, then again keeping close to it on its higher side until we reach the enclosed land and village of Jump, better known now as Roborough.

The meanderings in the fields of the border country, under roads and in covered conduits, would be too tedious to describe, but we find ourselves eventually in the delightful reservoir of Drake's Place[18], in the very centre of Plymouth, our fate from then on being quite unpredictable, our reward only to know we are there to serve the people.

Part 2. Death of a Dewdrop. *Period the 1980's.*

My rebirth has taken a rather different form. No frightening storm this time. Instead it is the calm of a midsummer night. Not a cloud in the sky. There is a full moon and the stars are brilliant. Such conditions give rise to a precipitation of moisture, which gently drips from fronds of grass, fern and bracken, providing some compensation from a long period of drought which has left the countryside dry and the rivers low. I am one of those dew-drops, more fortunate than many of my companions who, as dawn breaks and a rising sun warms the air, are drawn back again to form nebulous clouds in the summer sky. I drop into a tiny pool and slowly, just a little at a time form a rivulet. Then joining forces with other rivulets gradually gather volume and pace and even little sounds as we tumble over miniature waterfalls. By one of those quirks of fate, a chance in how many millions of millions, I find myself in that very same broad stony valley of Combeshead where I was born as a raindrop. In much the same way, but at a slower tempo and with fewer companions, we gather ourselves into a stream and descend through that little gorge beneath the tor, and assume the same name as before, Combeshead Brook.

That mysterious stone row is still there, looking more imposing now, for its fallen stones have all been re-erected[19]. They make a very brave sight as they stretch away into the hazy distance. But the tinner's heaps look no different, just as I remember them over a century and a half ago.

Ah. Yes. I remember those gerts in the hillside, where the caches are, and the little watercourse on the opposite bank. But I am disappointed to find that there is no water flowing into it now, the bed of the leat is quite dry, shallow, almost unrecognisable in places. And those caches, particularly the one that was so difficult to find, there is a well-worn path leading up to it now. The large one on the other side of the valley has a new entrance, blatantly obvious, not at all as I remember it. They must have frequent visitors.

What other surprises are in store for me? What about that water-wheel, will it still be turning? We come to the ford and the little clapper bridge. The track to Combeshead Farm seems to be still well-used, but not by anyone from the farm, for alas that is now but an empty shell, half of a pathetic window and a bit of the porch is all that is recognisable. The old storage cave in the courtyard contains no vegetables, only a discarded empty tin and a cigarette packet. How sad.

As we approach the Deancombe Brook I look for the tinner's mill, but all is silent there and I can see nothing but tall bracken where the water-wheel was. I know that the wheel-pit must still be there, some remains of the little house and perhaps a mortar stone or two. Lower down a bright green mire covers the low ground between the two brooks. It must be caused by water still oozing from the adit.

As the gentle flow of our combined streams descends beside the broad green meadows linking the farms of Combeshead and Deancombe, an ominous silence pervades the valley, broken only by the occasional bleat of a sheep and the song of the brook as it breaks over boulders, a song that lulls me to drowsiness. I sleep......and I dream.......

I see a funeral procession slowly wending its way down the green meadow. The cortege is headed by a column of bowler-hatted men in pairs, their heads bowed, hands clasped behind their backs, in reverence for the dead man who follows in his coffin carried on an old farm cart. Even the horse seems to sense the solemnity of the occasion. More figures follow the cart, and two more, somewhat separated from the rest, bring up the rear, one of them carrying a Gladstone bag. It is the year 1932, the body in the coffin is that of William Pengelly, aged 90, the last occupant of Combeshead Farm. The pathos of the picture is overwhelming, it marks the end of an era. With the passing of old William, the valley dies with him[20].

There is no use now for that sunken lane that climbs the hillside, no one will be going from here to Sheepstor Church any longer. With disuse the lane has become choked with trees, both living and dead, and is impassable.

I am awakened by the increased speed of the brook as it hastens over the rocky steepening descent in what is still one of the loveliest stretches of its course, a tree-lined glade where lie old Outcombe Farm and the blowing-house. The blowing-house is little changed, except that the crazing millstone has disappeared, perhaps to adorn someone's garden! A group of trees with an insecure footing on the river bank have been blown over and lie across the stream. They are still in leaf, they live on. Further down dead branches have been swept away by floods, then halted by boulders and form what is made to look like an otter's dam. We pass beneath it, and in a while come to Dennicombe Ford. No children play here now. The lower part of the old lane to the farm has become flooded with an overspill from the stream, to be joined where the lane turns and steepens, by the outflow from an adit nearby Deancombe Farm.

No one lives at Deancombe any more, the buildings are all in ruins. And not the buildings that I remember. Sir Massey Lopes, who bought all this land with the fortune he made on the sugar plantations in the West Indies, had the old farmstead rebuilt in 1858, but now even those buildings are mere shells. No haystacks now, but some of the staddles remain, their picturesque setting relieving the sombreness of the crumbling walls. The valley lane is trodden by many more feet now, visitors, hikers, letter-box hunters and parties of chattering children being taken to see those caches. In place of farm carts a Land Rover may bounce its way over the uneven surface, whilst overhead the silent vigil of wheeling buzzard or hovering kestrel is rudely disturbed by the sudden scream of a jet plane, setting nerves ajangle and pulse racing, the cacophony of sound persisting long after the plane is lost to view.

More sorrow and disappointment lies ahead. The lovingly remembered setting of our passage between the tors of Narrow and Snappers is unrecognisable, lost in a forest of closely packed conifers, the tors hidden from view, the name of the former forgotten. The canopy of the trees robs the valley of light, the dead branches of those that have been cut down by the foresters litter the ground and choke the stream, all is chaos and bewilderment.

Middleworth Farm is near lost in the trees, that charming old cottage, now reduced to a few low walls, has been replaced by another of Sir Massey's reconstructions, a gaunt cube of masonry looking more like the ruin of a castle keep than that of a farmhouse. That also is in ruins, the tops of its massive walls capped with cement to prevent further decay.

We get used to the gloom, and, here and there, when the sun breaks through the overhead mantle, our brook resumes its old appearance of charm and cheerfulness, but for the most part we are lost to the world.

As we approach the valley of the Mew, and I find I have now to call it the Meavy, we are in for another shock. A road crosses us on a quite elegant granite bridge carrying a road on which cars are passing. But beyond all is chaos and confusion again, and quite unknown to anyone our brook becomes lost, in fact ceases to exist, in a huge impersonal lake. The waters of Mew, Nillacombe and Narrator become inextricably mixed and form this reservoir. Drake's wonderful leat is no more. Where we had that frightening experience in the launder round the cliff edge at Beara Tor Gorge the valley is spanned by a massive dam, holding back our waters. Beautiful on the surface the lake may be, they call it Burrator now, and it attracts many visitors. But they do not see what we see below. No grassy meadow now, all is a uniform stretch of mud. Stumps of tree trunks stick up forlornly and hideously. The old leat course can still be traced and alongside it, between weir and Sheepstor Bridge, lies the outline of a cottage, Headweir Cottage it was, built by the Plymouth Corporation for Amos Shillabeer, son of William who accompanied us all those years ago[21]. Amos carried on the tradition of his father and grandfather by tending the needs of the reservoir.

The beautiful little Sheepstor Bridge, quite bare now of all its foliage, is perhaps the most pathetic sight of all, carrying nothing to nowhere, a forgotten and sunken monument of the bridge-builders of old, who, perhaps unconsciously, designed their bridges with taste and artistry. Traces of the old road lead away from it in both directions, to Sheepstor in one, to Walkhampton in the other. Where the latter road emerges from the waters the old tree-clad lane, known as Wembley Walk[22], houses a little museum of relics of the past, the work of the fourth generation of the Shillibeer family[23], another George, son of Amos, who was housed in a new building nearby the lane called 'The Lodge'. On the other side of the reservoir, in the grounds of Longstone Manor, are more relics; a group of troughs retrieved from various farms, a cheese press and a cider press. A more permanent reminder of the activities of that old building is a fine windstrew, a raised platform where the grain from the mill was threshed. A slotted gatepost still stands at the head of the lane going east to Norsworthy and Vennilake, whilst in the opposite

52. The stony lane leading from Deancombe Farm towards Down Tor, the quickest way to Nillacombe.

53. Remains of staddles at Deancombe Farm.

Photo: Western Morning News, 1932

54. A Moorman's funeral. The funeral procession of William Pengelly of Combeshead, 1932.

55. The old doorway of Roundypark Farm, flanked by two millstones from Longstone Manor. (Compare Hemery's picture 86, page 85, "High Dartmoor".)

56. Wembley Walk, where the younger George Shillibeer created a museum of farm relics. In the foreground, left, is a granite lectern from Longstone.

57. Doorway and plaques from Longstone Manor.

58. The old road to Sheepstor from Longstone.

direction, past the ruins of the old house, is the road to Sheepstor. With the water level low at this time of drought it is possible to walk along it.

Verily this is a sad tale of the passing of so many farms, a cemetery of ruined buildings. They have all come to an end since the reservoir was built in 1898, to safeguard the waters from pollution.

I have a presentiment that my end also is not far off. My wanderings round the lake cease as I approach the massive wall of the dam. Suddenly I find myself in a dark tunnel, no light of any sort filters through. I am confined in a large iron pipe. It is difficult to know how fast or how far we are travelling, or for how long we are to endure these dreadful conditions. We lose all sense of time and become reconciled to our fate, on and on and on.

Finally we emerge in a reservoir, very much smaller than Burrator. It is the Water Treatment Works at Crownhill, where we are passed through sludge lagoons, settling tanks and filters. Not satisfied with that the authorities dose us with chlorine. Thus purified we pass into Plymouth's distribution network. One thrill is vouchsafed us before we leave, the sight of a short section of Drake's Leat outside the main buildings, preserved in memory of a great undertaking, the neat granite lined banks a monument to the final maintenance of this historic leat [24].

I am directed into a very very old pipe, so old that some of the joints have given way. I find myself escaping through one of the leaks. But it is no escape.....I am caught in mud and slime.....I suffocate...can no longer move....I, I am just mud beneath the pavements of Plymouth. It is the end. I..I........

* * * * *

Poor dear Dewdrop. Shed a tear for his passing. He did so love that beautiful valley, the gay sparkle of the waters, the green of the trees and meadows, and the remembrance of all those people he met.

What will he find if he comes back again, in whatever form, in another hundred and fifty years? Oh no. No. Not that. It is too horrible to contemplate. A blackened, treeless, featureless landscape, devastated by a nuclear bomb? No. Not that dear God. Not that.

Notes and References

1. Streaming for tin in olden times involved a lot more than panning the deposits in the beds of streams. The formation of alluvial and eluvial tin in valleys occurred in very ancient geological times. Subsequent climatic changes such as the ice ages resulted in the tin ground being covered by a variety of deposits. In R. D. Penhallurick's 'TIN in ANTIQUITY' p.158 he instances streamworks in the Roche Parish in Cornwall having an overburden of 6 metres above tin ground 9.1 metres thick. Such or similar conditions occurred on Dartmoor, resulting in the steep scarps, sometimes very widely separated, which line the tin workings in the upper valleys.
2. Crossing's 'GUIDE', p.449 and Eric Hemery's 'HIGH DARTMOOR', p.149.
3. Hemery p.150.
4. Crossing p.449.
5. Hemery p.152 and described in detail by Dr. Tom Greeves in TDA 101 of 1969. William Pryce (Mineralogia Cornubiensis, 1778) describes a buddle as "Pits dug in the earth near the stamping mill, seven feet long, three feet wide, and two and a half feet deep, where the stamped tin is curiously washed from its impurities by water constantly running through the buddle, while a boy, called a buddle boy, is standing in the body of it, and working both with a shovel and with his feet."
6. Hemery pp.156/157 and Worth's 'DARTMOOR' p.308.
7. Hemery p.143.
8. Hemery p.157.
9. Shown as such on first edition of OS one-inch map Sheet 90 dated 1809.
10. Hemery p.159.
11. Actually Newlycombe Lake but so pronounced by moormen.
12. Hemery p.178.
13. David Hawkings' 'WATER FROM THE MOOR' p.73.
14. Robert Burnard's 'DARTMOOR PICTORIAL RECORDS' part IV pp.64/65 for a charming picture of it.
15. Hawkings pages 9, 11 and 17.
16. Crispin Gill's 'PLYMOUTH' Vol.2 pages 80, 118, 128, 138.
17. Hemery's 'WALKING THE DARTMOOR RAILROADS' p.17.
18. As very young boys, my brother Dennis and I travelled to school by train, from Plymouth's Milbay Station to Devonport Halt. The local train always left at the same time and from the same platform, until one day some alteration had been made and instead of Devonport Halt we found ourselves at Plymouth North Road Station. We had no idea how we could find our way to school from there and decided we would walk to Drake's Place Reservoir and there play until it was time to go home to lunch. On the lower side of the reservoir a colonnaded shelter with seats faces an area of grass and garden, a pleasant spot to enjoy three hours of idleness. This is a firmly implanted childhood memory, no doubt because it is accompanied by a sense of guilt.

    In those days the water arrived at the reservoir in the form of two splendid fountains.
19. Burnard, part IV p.69. He writes:

    "The monuments commence at the western end with a sepulchral circle, having an inside diameter of thirty-seven feet. In this is a small barrow, which has been dug into by some seeker after treasure. This circle is the starting point of a fine single Row of upright stones, which extends in a straight line nearly six hundred yards in length, eastly, and terminates in the direction of a fine cairn which shows signs of chambering. The Row consists of one hundred and seventy-three visible stones. The majority of these have fallen, including the two fine specimens at the extreme west end, close to the circle. With the kind permission of Sir Massey Lopes, Bart., these two and a smaller one, lying a few feet east of them, were on April 14th, 1894, re-erected by the Messrs. Turpin, of Plymouth, under the instructions and superintendence of the Rev. S. Baring-Gould, the Rev. W. A. Gray, and the author.

The largest stone is twelve feet ten inches long, and weighs about three tons. It now stands nine feet above the level of the ground.

The illustration shows this stone erect and in process of being secured by tamping, whilst the second is being slung prior to being placed in position.

The holes dug in the "calm", in which these stones formerly stood, were very apparent on clearing the ground, so that they occupy their exact original position.

On July 6th, 7th and 9th, 1894, all the fallen stones were re-erected in their original sockets, making the Row one of the most perfect of its kind on Dartmoor."

20. Rev. Hugh Breton, 'FOREST OF DARTMOOR' Part 2.
21. Hawkings Plate 24 p.33.
22. Hemery p.116.
23. He built two arches across the lane and in between them a series of rockeries, alternating from side to side, so that the path snakes between them. In the lower arch, which has a castellated top, he incorporated a fine doorway from Longstone Manor, above it the letter E representing the Elford family, and on each side of it other commemorative plaques with dates of 1637 and 1633.

    The upper arch also incorporates an old doorway, this from Roundypark Farm, near Crazywell Pool. The initials PC and date 1668, above the arch may possibly refer to the date when Phillip Cockle rebuilt his farm. (Both Crossing and Hemery have read the initials as RC, Crossing assuming they stood for Richard Crymes, and Hemery as those of Ralph Cockle. My photograph of the doorway makes it quite clear that the first letter is a P, the full-stop after the P could easily have made it look like an R in poor light or if disguised by moss. Hemery's recording of details of tenancy at the farm, p.142, make Philip Cockle quite a possibility.) On each side of the doorway, incorporated in the wall, is a millstone from Longstone Manor. On the higher side of this arch lies an inscribed stone, removed from Headweir Cottage when that building was demolished, and on the other side of it two other stones recording the date when Sir Massey Lopes rebuilt Deancombe Farm, ML 1858, and possibly Middleworth ML 1870. Nearer the lower arch is an altogether different relic, a lectern from Longstone Manor, which suggests that a chapel was at one time incorporated in the building. At the top of the lane a mortar stone with two hollows came from a blowing-house now also submerged beneath the reservoir. (see Worth's 'DARTMOOR' p.305, who states that two mould stones were once here, but these have disappeared.)

    Much moss had to be removed from the stones before I could record them. The lane is sadly neglected and not open to the public. I am grateful to Mr. Taylor of Burrator Lodge for permission to photograph these objects.
24. Hawkings Plate 9, p.15.

Index